Man Trap

Also by Gwen Moffat

Lady with a Cool Eye
Deviant Death
The Corpse Road
Miss Pink at the Edge of the World
Hard Option
Over the Sea to Death
A Short Time to Live
Persons Unknown
The Buckskin Girl
Die Like a Dog
Last Chance Country
Grizzly Trail
Snare
The Stone Hawk
Rage
The Raptor Zone
Pit Bull
Veronica's Sisters
The Outside Edge
Cue the Battered Wife
A Wreath of Dead Moths
The Lost Girls
Running Dogs
Private Sins
Quicksand
Retribution

Non-fiction

Space Below my Feet
Two Star Red
On my Home Ground
Survival Count
Hard Road West
The Storm Seekers

MAN TRAP

Gwen Moffat

Constable • London

First published in Great Britain 2003
by Constable, an imprint of Constable & Robinson Ltd
3 The Lanchesters, 162 Fulham Palace Road,
London W6 9ER
www.constablerobinson.com

ISBN 1–84119–699–1

Printed and bound in Great Britain

A CIP catalogue record for this book
is available from the British Library

Chapter One

'She's only fifteen,' Ruth Ogilvie protested. 'And when was I ever hysterical? Come off it, Charlie, if you had children you might have some idea . . . I'm sorry, I'm just saying it's freezing hard and I reckon she's gone out in only a fleece and trainers. I know she hasn't –'

'But she didn't go on her bike –'

'I said! It's still in the shed. I tell you, she's been picked up –'

'By arrangement then. No one's going to be driving past your road-end by chance on a winter's night. She's with one of her school pals. There are plenty of lads with cars.' There was a pause, Charlie Innes thinking that cars owned by local youngsters were mostly lethal old bangers.

Ruth gripped the phone and stared at the calendar, today's date marked with the instruction: 'Mum. Dentist 5 p.m.' 'I was home by six thirty,' she said. 'She didn't even leave a note.'

'Look, love, she's old enough to take care of herself, she knows all the boys; we know their parents, for God's sake! It's not as if it's summer with dodgy characters around –'

'*That* never crossed my mind.' It had but she'd dismissed it before speculation might remind her that rape was often perpetrated by people you knew. 'I was thinking of accidents,' she went on heatedly. 'Black ice, hairpin bends . . . He could – how many of the local boys drive carefully at any time, let alone on a night like this, the deer all over the road? It's *eleven*, Charlie!'

'I'll come up and keep you company and bring a bottle.'

'I have to look for her –'

'You don't know where they are –'

'They won't have left the glen.'

'They're not going to be driving around. They're in a house – in someone's house, I mean – at a party.' He was reaching, her panic getting to him. 'You've rung her friends?'

'What good would that do? You remember last time. If she's just being – assertive . . .' She trailed off.

'Did you quarrel at breakfast time?'

'Not at all. Anyway, it doesn't need a quarrel; everything I do – everything I say – is wrong nowadays.'

'She's at that age. You stay there; I'll be with you shortly.'

Charlie didn't mind turning out at eleven on a February night, on the contrary he welcomed the excuse. When Ruth Ogilvie moved into her cottage a year ago initially she'd been of no interest to him; just another single mother with a teenage daughter: no background, no skills other than that of cleaning people's houses. But the daughter was startlingly pretty and, seeing them together in the supermarket, Charlie was suddenly aware of the similarity between them, and realized that the mother was something more than pretty. He had stared, she had turned and he found himself trying to determine the colour of her eyes. Green? Pale green verging on grey, or blue-grey? She had smiled, taking the initiative.

'Have we met?'

Apologizing, he'd introduced himself as their neighbour – well, a few miles away: neighbours in this remote Highland glen. That was last March, eleven months ago, and now not a day went by without his thinking about her: planning, even plotting how, when, to acquaint her with his feelings, his intentions.

Charlie was an old career soldier. Never married, the Army his mistress, once retired he had come back to his roots in the Grampian hills and tried to fill the gaping void in his life by tending his garden, cooking his own vegetables and making wine. Then Ruth came into his life and his prospects changed – he *had* prospects again – but he was made aware almost at once that it wasn't the mother he would have to win over but the daughter. Without a father Heather was rebellious and possessive; it was the worst time for a strange man to enter her mother's life. So Charlie dreamed and waited and adored his lady without (he thought) her ever knowing what was in his mind. Ruth knew but gave no sign; privately she had considered marrying him but was well aware that Heather's hostility must be overcome first. The girl had no doubts concerning Charlie's intentions and treated him as rudely as she dared.

The situation was fraught, then, when Charlie, driving carefully up the glen this bitter night, watching for black ice, alert for deer, saw a figure in his headlights. He dipped the beams but not before she turned, shielding her eyes. He grimaced at his own thoughts: relief at finding her unharmed but disappointment that he was not to have Ruth to himself for a while. He stopped and she climbed in, admitting a blast of freezing air.

'Jesus!' she gasped. 'It's fucking cold out there.'

'New recruits talk like that,' he said amiably. 'They feel they need to make an impression. Walked far?'

'Far enough.'

'It's turned eleven. Ruth's climbing the wall.'

'So?'

A pause. 'Been thrown out of a car?'

'How d'you –' She bit it off. '*I* left *him*,' she said coldly.

'You didn't leave a note saying when you intended coming home.'

'What's it to you?'

'I'd be one of the searchers looking for your body.'

She gave a derisive snort. 'You figure I'd be a murder victim? This is real life, not television.'

'I wasn't thinking in those terms. Up here it's blizzards and hypothermia you have to contend with, not boys.'

'I wasn't with a boy.'

That silenced him. It rang true and he didn't like it.

'She smothers me,' Heather said sullenly.

'Anyone would worry on a winter's night and not knowing where you are.'

'I can take care of myself.'

'That's what I told her.'

He was slowing for the last familiar bend, creeping round, indicating out of habit although there was nothing on the road apart from his Range Rover. He turned through a gateway where the sagging gate and the mail box were draped with snow. The 'Rover crawled up the frozen ruts in low gear, crystals sparkling in the headlights. Above, a yellow gleam appeared like a low star. He suppressed a sigh. For him this high croft, the last occupied house in the glen, epitomized the indomitable spirit of human settlement in a land that was both beautiful and bleak. He knew he was a romantic; to practical Ruth this cottage was no more than shelter: somewhere to raise her daughter. It was four walls, a roof, warmth and dry beds. He wondered what it meant to Heather.

The front door was open, Ruth a silhouette against the light, waiting for the car to stop. When her daughter approached, Charlie, stumbling round the bonnet, was afraid of what might happen, the girl advancing so grimly, the mother like a rock in her path, but Ruth moved aside and Heather brushed past her. Ruth turned to follow and Charlie entered, closing the door with exaggerated care.

In the kitchen Heather went straight to the fridge collecting cheese, pickles, Flora. 'I'm starving,' she announced. 'Isn't there any soup?'

Ruth's face was drawn with tension, tight lips parted and stretched as if words had been strangled. Charlie moved to intercept her fixed stare and shook his head warningly. He placed a bottle of Lochnagar on the table. 'Glasses?' he suggested.

Ruth came to life. 'Where did you find her?'

He sagged a little. 'First things first,' he murmured, and stepped to a cupboard, reaching for glasses. Ruth's glare focused on the third glass. At the draining board Heather was trying to open a can of soup. 'Let me,' Charlie urged. 'Pour the whisky, Ruth; her hands are numb. She's been walking in the snow. No gloves. Let's get some warmth into her.'

Ruth's expression changed from rage to concern. She swooped for a saucepan, clattered it noisily on the stove, threw open the fire door. 'You've been *walking* –' Her eyes fastened on the girl's feet. 'Get those trainers off, and your jeans: look, they're soaked! Why? What happened?'

'You see?' Heather addressed Charlie: 'She smothers.'

Ruth was immobile, tense again. Charlie emptied the soup into the pan. 'Who were you with?' Ruth asked on a high note, struggling to sound casual.

Her daughter sat down and tried to unlace her trainers but the knots were frozen tight and her fingers stiff. Ruth dropped to the floor.

'Don't!' Heather shouted. 'Don't help me! I don't *need* you!'

Ruth jerked back on her heels as the girl leapt to her feet and blundered out of the kitchen. They heard her pound up the stairs and a door slammed. A whisper of dust dropped from the ceiling. Charlie helped Ruth to her feet. She sank into a chair and reached for the whisky. He said nothing, taking refuge in his own drink, waiting for her to collect herself, ready with comfort, reassurance, whatever was needed. He understood that all adolescents went through a difficult phase; it hadn't happened with him, nor to his contemporaries, but the world was different today. Children grew up too quickly, desires and aspirations outstripped experience. Today's media melodramas were grafted on the myth that youth was inviolate, and the result was a brash swagger that would disappear along with puberty. He said so.

'In another year she'll be so preoccupied with exams that

you won't be able to prise her away from her books – or computer, if that's how they revise nowadays.'

Ruth regarded him distractedly. 'Did she say who she was with?'

He decided to play it carefully, she'd had enough trouble tonight. 'Whoever it was, she left him. A difference of opinion . . .' He stopped, seeing where that was leading, but so had Ruth.

'At least she resisted – apparently. Her trainers hadn't come off.' She laughed harshly.

'She's home, love.'

She glowered, then gasped. 'She should be in a hot bath! D'you think she's getting out of those wet clothes?' She made to rise.

'No! Leave her. She knows what to do, she's not a baby. She'll come round, you know. She was trying to get things back to normal when she came in.'

'And I ruined it, that's what you're implying. Look at the time, Charlie! She's been out on the road on a night like this; between rape and pregnancy, murder, a car smash, a blizzard – how d'you expect me to behave when she comes in close to midnight and says she's hungry?'

'I can cope.' Charlie's eyes widened at his own words.

'You don't have to. You're only a neighbour; a friend, yes, but you don't have it all the time.'

'I should. I mean . . .' He wavered as the pale eyes turned on him. 'She needs a father,' he said staunchly. 'A stepfather certainly but I do know something about young people; I saw enough raw recruits in the Army.' She said nothing. 'If you'll have me.' It was almost defiant, certainly not humble. 'Of course,' he added, 'I'm not asking you to marry me because Heather needs a father. The priority is yourself, but I'm happy to have a ready-made family as it were. You don't look surprised; did you suspect how I feel?'

At last she smiled. 'You wear your heart on your sleeve, my dear.' No way was she going to tell him that Heather had derided his intentions in the crudest terms. 'I'm only surprised at the timing. It's been a wild evening, but then drama does tend to escalate. Let me think about it – and don't say anything' – she glanced at the ceiling – 'she remembers her father too clearly, or says she does; after all she was only five . . .' Ruth's husband had electrocuted himself with an inspection lamp while working under his car. 'It's not only the dying but the horror of a violent death,' she went on. 'Particularly for a child, and she did see him there, even if she thought he was asleep. Thank God she didn't touch him. But you see, only ten years ago . . . We're good friends, Charlie, so let's leave it like that – for the time being. It won't be long before she's in college.'

Fat chance of that, he thought resentfully, envisioning the years he'd have to wait before Ruth would allow herself to be more than a good friend. And Heather was never going to make college the way she was behaving; if she was graduating to men at fifteen she certainly wasn't going to revert to boys.

'Now what?' Ruth asked. 'You look like thunder.'

He licked his lips. She ought to know. 'She wasn't with a boy.'

'She *was* walking – all this time? Never.'

'She was with someone. She said it wasn't a boy.'

Ruth filled her glass half-way and drank, not sipping. She wouldn't look at him.

'You know who it is,' he stated. 'Who?'

She exhaled heavily. 'Randal Gow. I didn't want you to know. I feel so inadequate.'

He ignored the last part of that. 'You're sure? How long has that been going on? He's twenty-two! They're not –' He stopped, his eyes narrowed. 'Does Caspar know?'

'We haven't discussed it.' Ruth's tone was dry. 'More to the point, does Milly? This is her cottage. The whole estate's hers.' She grinned without humour. 'Milly doesn't know. If she did we'd have been evicted as soon as she found out.'

'Oh, come on, Ruth; you're not her tenant.'

'Worse, we're here on sufferance. You think she'd stay friendly if she knew her son was dating an under-age girl? If we were paying rent there'd be a contract. As a grace-and-favour occupant I'd be out on my ear as soon as she discovered what her son was up to.'

'Rubbish. You'd come to me. No, don't argue, you'll never be homeless while I'm around. And what's happening has to be Randal's doing; he's the adult – although hardly mature in my opinion. How did you find out? Did Heather tell you or did you find –'

'Did I find her diary? No, I've not sunk to that level. She told me. And of course' – seeing his surprise – 'when I pointed out that she was under age, she accused me of having a dirty mind.' Ruth gestured angrily. 'She says they just drive. They don't go anywhere, they drive. How long has it been going on? I don't know. How often do they meet? I don't know. Sometimes she says one thing, sometimes another. She contradicts herself and doesn't care.' She studied her drink. 'She comes out with the wildest announcements,' she went on miserably: 'says she can marry in a year's time, without actually saying, but implying that it would be Randal –'

'She would still need –'

'She even said, "When I'm mistress of Blair I can make that place pay." I was so amazed that she had the grace to back down and say she meant *if* she were mistress of Blair.'

'She's winding you up, that's all.'

'Of course, but if I were to come straight out and accuse her of fantasy, she'd take that as retaliation and matters would escalate.' He was puzzled. 'What?' she barked. 'You think we need professional help?' Sardonic now.

'I'm thinking that it mightn't be fantasy, that it could have some foundation. Randal might have mentioned marriage, even referred to his inheritance. "Mistress of Blair"? I don't see that originating with Heather.'

'I can't imagine Randal using it.'

'Lamont would. Heather's friendly with Hayley

Lamont. "Mistress of Blair". It has a seductive ring. Funny thing, it emphasizes Milly's status; she's the landowner, not Caspar.'

'He's making full use of her money though.' Ruth was grim. 'The way he's operating there can't be much cash left. The cascade has to be costing a bomb.'

'The bank will be paying. These big landowners have all their wealth tied up in property. Milly's always selling a house here, a few acres of woodland there; that's how I came to acquire a keeper's cottage. Blair has one gamekeeper now where ten years ago they had four.'

'But Milly lets me have this place rent-free, and we never met until I traded on the fact that my husband used to service Caspar's Bentley – hers really of course.'

'She likes you; she admires you as the gallant widow going out to work.' His eyes softened, making a fond joke of it. 'As for this place, no other woman would live out here and you're keeping it aired, stopping it from falling down. The rent would be peanuts to Milly anyway, relative to Blair's overdraft.'

'Then why are they going deeper into debt with this crazy water feature?'

'Caspar's philosophy is that you spend money to make it. He was in the City, remember: investments. Although he couldn't have been much good at it or he'd have stayed there. But then he married Milly: a rich heiress – well, as far as property's concerned, and no doubt he saw Blair as a potential goldmine. And there again, as the occupier of the castle, if not the owner, he has status. Caspar's strong on status. The water garden is a case in point. He's modelling it on Chatsworth's; he's going to outshine Balmoral.'

'Balmoral doesn't have gardens, as such.'

'It has the Queen. And Blair will have Caspar in full Highland fig, playing the Lord of Blair.'

'I didn't realize you dislike him so much.'

'Nor did I until tonight. He's a charlatan and a wannabe and he's raised his son in his own image.'

'Milly dotes on him, on both of them, and be fair, Charlie, they have tremendous charm: father and son.'

'That's the trouble. Caspar seduced Milly, now the son has – charmed your daughter.'

Ruth missed the hesitation and sighed. 'I'm going to have to find an excuse to talk to Milly.' She glanced round the kitchen. 'That should be easy enough; I can take my pick of draughts and leaks, something that has to be fixed after the snow melts. Once we're talking I can raise the subject of Randal.' She looked doubtful. 'Don't you think? Awkward, isn't it?'

Chapter Two

To the uninitiated, old Highland properties can appear exquisitely romantic. Croft houses such as Ruth's nestle against their rock-strewn slopes as if they've grown there which, in a sense, they have, being built of stone quarried close by. Blair Essan, on the other hand: an old tower house, its turrets and pepperpot roofs embellished with Victorian crow steps and crenellations – Blair was impressive rather than exquisite, and only the occupiers of these houses knew the reality behind the façades: damp and draughts and dodgy plumbing. All Blair's flaws would be eradicated of course, once the owners had tapped the lucrative tourist market: the gardens put in order, the cascade completed, the house – ah yes, the house . . . In spring all its windows would be opened to the balmy air, the damp dried out, unsightly patches plastered, the best furniture transferred to the great hall to create an impact as visitors entered by the front door. The Farquharson was intended to occupy the space where the William Morris had hung: that tapestry which was now the focal point in a drawing room looking out over Central Park in New York.

This morning Caspar and Millicent Gow were in the hall, both in chunky sweaters, cords and sheepskin boots, a middle-aged couple fitting their environment: Caspar tall and lean with the austere and aquiline look of landed gentry, Millicent big-boned and plain but with undoubted presence, the product of generations of women who had been chatelaines of Blair castle. At this moment neither was authoritative nor cool; they were bewildered but where Milly was at a loss, Caspar was furious.

'If we had security it couldn't have happened,' he blustered.

'I can't think how they did it.' Milly was shaking her head. 'And why, Caspar? It's five feet high and nearly that wide . . . And how did they know it was there, in that passage? And why take it in the first place? There are far more valuable objects lying around.'

'Where?'

'I don't know.' She looked about her helplessly. 'Nothing's in tip-top condition – but why *that*? What's it worth?'

'Thousands. Five figures to Americans.' It was a wild guess. 'And how d'you know they haven't taken anything else?'

'We have to look – Oh, Lord, here's Ruth.' The dogs were barking on the forecourt and an old Land Rover passed a window, the sound of its engine muted by thick stone and the great timbered door.

'Someone knew it was there,' Caspar hissed, staring at the window.

'We have to report it.' Suddenly Milly was firm. 'It'll be insured of course; Daddy was always most particular about insurance.' She crossed to the door. Caspar, still muttering angrily, retreated, leaving her to cope with the visitor.

Ruth came in, shouldered by boisterous Labradors, herself in a puffer jacket and the ubiquitous sheepskin boots. Exchanging small talk on the weather, on the temperature last night, the likelihood and the timing of the next snowfall, they moved along a flagged passage to the kitchen, its door closed to keep in the heat. The atmosphere was a benediction once they entered, both moving automatically to the Aga, Milly pushing the kettle over to a hotplate. 'The Farquharson's missing,' she announced.

Ruth stared. 'The what?'

'A painting by Joseph Farquharson. It hung in the passage leading to the stable yard. Caspar said it had to go in the hall for when we open the house, but when we went to see if we could move it ourselves, it was gone.'

'You mean you've been burgled? Of course you do. When did it happen?'

Milly sighed and brought mugs to the table. 'Who knows? Neither of us can remember when we were last there. The passage leads to old store rooms and an outside door that's locked and bolted at night. The women go down there to clean but I have no need to; anyway, would you notice? It's huge certainly, virtually five feet square, but it's – it was in a dim passage. In a place like this – uneven stone floors – you're watching your feet, not looking at the walls. Caspar would go out that way to the stable but he'd not notice it was missing.'

'Someone must have known it was there.' Ruth slipped out of her jacket and hung it over the back of a chair. She sat down and regarded Milly thoughtfully. The other woman was pouring water on coffee granules, seemingly concentrating on the job in hand. Ruth wondered what was going on in her mind. 'An inside job?' she hazarded. 'You've considered it.' She thought it obvious.

'People have been in and out,' Milly admitted vaguely. 'There's a lavatory just inside that back door and the men who were building the cascade used it when the one in the stables froze up. Any of them could have taken a few steps down the passage out of curiosity – and everyone in these parts knows a Farquharson.'

'I don't.'

'You're not a local, Ruth. Joseph Farquharson was laird of Finzean on Deeside. He did Landseer-type stuff – you know: like the stag at bay, only Farquharson did sheep. Actually this one isn't sheep; it's just a bit of woodland and snow. I'll show you a photo. The style must have been fashionable in the nineteenth century, which will be why we came to acquire it.'

Ruth smiled at the pronoun; Millie was in her fifties and

it had to be some great-grandparent who she was referring to. 'Does it have any value?' she asked.

'I've no idea. It's insured although goodness knows what it's valued at. Caspar says thousands but that's wishful thinking. It did occur to me some time ago that it's probably worth more than five hundred, and someone on the television said you should take photographs of valuables so I went round one afternoon snapping everything that I thought might fetch more than five hundred pounds. Now I can impress the police with a picture.' She nodded smugly.

'What does Caspar say?'

'He's absolutely livid, my dear.'

'How did they get in, Milly? The burglars?'

Milly spread her hands. 'You arrived as we were speculating. Caspar's gone to look around, I suppose. No doubt it was something like a broken window latch. It can't have been a door . . .' She trailed off. There was no need to complete it. In Glen Essan, particularly in the depths of winter, people were slack about locking doors at night.

'Besides,' Ruth pointed out, 'there are the dogs.'

'Yes, the dogs never barked. Oh!' They laughed, both devotees of Conan Doyle. They sobered as quickly, remembering why that dog didn't bark in the night.

Milly said, 'If it was an inside job it wasn't one of the women. It must weigh a ton. All the frames on these Victorian pictures do.'

'Women have menfolk – and you said yourself: there were the workmen.'

'Still are, of course, except that they can't work on the cascade until the snow melts.' She sighed. 'As if Caspar doesn't have enough on his hands: the water feature, all the channels to be dug, the dam, the landscaping . . . he's going to be pushed for time and he's determined to open in June. There are bound to be teething troubles even if the Queen doesn't come till August.'

'The Queen! What's this?'

Milly was embarrassed. 'He's going to ask her to open the grounds formally.'

Ruth gulped and said quickly, 'Why, that'll be a terrific boost for you – for the business: an endorsement.' Caspar, she thought wildly, had to be making a bid for a peerage.

The man himself opened the door then, his dogs slipping through with him. He greeted Ruth pleasantly, evidently recovered from his anger, apparently unfazed: the country gentleman dealing competently with a minor problem. 'No sign that I can see of a break-in,' he told his wife. 'The police may discover something. Fingerprints maybe. My money's on that door into the yard.'

'It should be locked and bolted at night,' Milly pointed out.

'Then – a ladder? An upstairs window? Not all the latches will be secure, an old place like this.'

'The dogs didn't bark.'

'Now how do we know that? Anyone could have entered when we were all out one evening. Where is Randy, by the way?'

Ruth stiffened, recalling the reason for her visit but unwilling to raise the subject while the father was present. Milly she could cope with: mother to mother; Caspar was an unknown quantity particularly now with Randal's coming down from Edinburgh under some unspecified cloud – that is, unspecified as far as Ruth knew. Now, thinking of Heather, she was wondering if that problem might have sinister connotations. Could Randal be involved with drugs? She clamped down on rising panic.

'He went to town.' Milly was dismissive. 'You have reported the theft to the police? Are they sending someone?'

He nodded and glanced at the kettle. 'We'll offer them coffee.' He smiled at Ruth. 'And a dram. Get them on our side.'

She blinked. Why shouldn't the police be on his side? To her relief he turned and went back to the front of the house. Now was the moment. 'I'm grateful to Randal,' she began warmly but in a rush and, seeing Milly's attempt to reorientate herself: 'For giving Heather a lift last night. She was only in trainers, would you believe, in all this snow?'

'He didn't say anything.' Milly spoke slowly. 'Where was he? He came home late – I think. You can't hear a car through these thick walls.'

'Charlie Innes picked her up sometime after eleven.' Ruth tried to steady her voice, as if fifteen-year-old girls made a habit of walking alone on snowy nights. 'Where she'd been I have no idea. They never tell you anything, do they?'

Their eyes met, Ruth forcing herself to appear naive, increasing wariness in Milly's face. Her eyes were her best feature: large, grey, expressive. Before that knowledgeable regard Ruth wilted, not defeated but helpless. 'I can't cope with her,' she admitted miserably.

'I'll speak to Randal,' Milly said, adding brightly, perhaps in an effort to divert Ruth from her son's behaviour, not to speak of his presence at home during term time: 'How did Charlie Innes come to be on the road so late? Was there something happening in the village?'

'He was on his way to my place.' Resentment built in Ruth, she had known this wasn't going to be an easy scene. 'I'd come home from the dentist to find the house empty and no note. So I phoned Charlie. I needed company, reassurance.' She was defiant, she shouldn't have to justify her actions. 'You hear such ghastly things.'

Milly said nothing but her eyes spoke for her. In a flash of intuition Ruth saw that she was frightened too. 'I didn't know who she was with,' she stressed. 'But Heather does fantasize. She has a crush on him.' It was verbal shorthand, a distillation of her fears.

'What does she say?' Milly had interpreted the shorthand correctly. Did she know – suspect?

'She says they drive around' – anger rose – 'and that if

I'm implying anything more, then that's my dirty mind. She makes jokes – about this place.'

'What kind of jokes?'

'It's a serious crush, Milly. She mentions marriage.' Ruth rushed on in an effort to blunt the impact: 'Charlie says she'll grow out of it with puberty – whenever a child is supposed to be finished with that!' She paused, aware of the other's reaction, momentarily forgetting thoughts of eviction, even of Heather. 'Milly, you look shattered! It's worrying for both of us, I know, but I'm sure Randal can be – is a sensible chap . . . I mean, it's not as if he doesn't know her age.' Ruth swallowed and hesitated. 'I hadn't considered what a shock it would be for you, I was too concerned about Heather. I'm sorry.' She was sincere, realizing that the possible consequences of their children's behaviour could be worse for Randal than for Heather. An abortion would be the long-stop for a girl – an under-age girl, but for the man the liaison could mean prison and the end of his career. 'I've gone off at half-cock,' she confessed. 'My panic's infected you.'

Milly made a sound that was suspiciously like a sob and clapped her hands to her mouth. Her eyes darted to the door. 'Someone's arrived,' she blurted, although Ruth had heard nothing. 'They're going to need coffee and a dram, Casper said. God, I could do with a dram, couldn't you?'

About to demur, then remembering this woman had just discovered a burglary, with all the shock that that entailed, Ruth agreed that whisky would be welcome. And then she thought what a relief it was that the police had been summoned in respect of a stolen painting. Twelve hours ago, waiting and worrying over Heather's unexplained absence, she had been forced to consider summoning them for something so hideous she could no longer name it even in her mind. Last night she'd been hysterical; Heather was right, she smothered her daughter. It was a schoolgirl crush, nothing more; no doubt Randal had been amused initially but now he could be looking for a chance to bow out of the situation. Milly would take care of it, probably send him back to Edinburgh – to his lodgings anyway. What could be wrong at the university?

'Come and give me moral support,' Milly ordered, heading for the door.

Ruth followed, feeling exhausted by emotion but relieved that this woman, whom she liked and respected, continued to accept her, didn't blame her for any actions of a wilful daughter. In the hall they found Caspar in conversation with Tom Malcolm, the local sergeant, and Milly was asked if anything were missing from her personal possessions, notably jewellery. Ruth went with her to her bedroom and the result of that was surprising enough that when she finally escaped from the castle, she went straight to Charlie Innes.

Cougar, the former keeper's cottage, was about two miles from the castle: a little house with gingerbread barge-boards, a few acres of snowy pastureland in front, a belt of hardwoods climbing a steep slope at the back. The access road was private, the surface marked by tyres, but they'd be those of Charlie's Range Rover. The site was as isolated as Ruth's croft but the trees lent it a more cosy ambience, those and the fenced fields, the dog pens – empty now – and a clutch of brown hens scratching in the stable yard. A drift of smoke rose from a chimney and there was a pungent smell of peat.

Over bacon sandwiches she told him about the burglary – all of it, because a pair of Milly's ear-rings was missing. 'What a nerve he had, Charlie! To go into their bedroom! And no one would have known, Milly wouldn't have known; after all, when does she ever wear jewellery, and certainly not those ear-rings? They dangle. She's not a dangly lady, is she? Ear-studs are Milly's mark. Caspar was furious.'

'Anyone would be.'

'Well, he was mad about the picture. She never told him she'd taken photographs; she'd thought nothing of it at the time, she was just playing with a new camera.'

'What else is missing of the jewellery?'

'Nothing. The good stuff's at the bank and she hasn't much at home but there were these agate ear-rings. She photographed them because she thought they might be worth a bit. They are rather beautiful, even in a snapshot; the stones have been cut on the cross so they're striped with different shades of brown, and set in gold. Antique, of course: an heirloom. Worth more than the painting, judging by the photo she took of that: just trees and snow and some rabbits.'

'*Afterglow*,' Charlie murmured. 'It's a print.'

'Hell, Charlie, this is Blair we're talking about. It's an original.'

'Then it's not *Afterglow*. That's in Aberdeen Art Gallery.'

'And it's huge: five feet tall; you wouldn't make a print that big, would you?'

'It's something else. He was a prolific man. That's a Farquharson in the parlour.' He got up and left the kitchen to return with a small framed picture. 'Now that is a print,' he said, handing it to her. 'Naturally. I couldn't possibly afford an original.'

'Really? That means the one at Blair is valuable? How much would it fetch?'

'I don't know what a big Farquharson would make these days. To a rich American enthusiast: five figures perhaps.'

'So someone not only knew it was there but knew it was valuable.' She studied his picture. 'I never really looked at this before. You have so much clutter in that room – not that it's untidy, mind, it's just that there's too much to look at . . . But this is beautiful! Look at the snow! And the shadow of the sheep – and that's a path under the bank, isn't it, all drifted, but you can see the indentation where the snow's settled.'

'I feel I'm there.' Charlie's eyes shone. 'The sun just showing over the ridge, that far slope catching the first light . . . I adore it.'

'It's far better than the one at Blair, but then, a Polaroid: the original is probably superior.'

'Well, *Afterglow* in Aberdeen is to my mind the finest of his paintings. You actually *experience* the cold. It's almost too real: uncomfortable.' He grinned. 'An odd thing about it: the footsteps in the snow are wrong, the chap who made them appears to have had two right feet. But then no one's perfect.' He took back the picture, squinted at it and sighed with pleasure. 'So what's the next move in this saga?'

'I wouldn't know, having left before the CID arrived. Tom Malcolm says that a van must have been used, you couldn't get a thing that size in a car. I reckon you could get it in the back of a Land Rover though. I didn't say so. I left them all going over the place looking to see if any furniture or ornaments were missing.' Her face changed. 'I feel a worm, Charlie; I tackled Milly about Heather and Randal.'

He gaped. 'After everything else?'

'It came up before the police arrived.' Ruth was shamefaced. 'We were suddenly alone in the kitchen and Caspar had just been in and asked where Randal was, and that reminded me of last night, so I told Milly how much I appreciated Randal giving Heather a lift in the snow.'

'But he didn't –'

'It was a gambit, to start the ball rolling. Milly was stunned; I swear she had no idea of the relationship – well, she could have suspected there was a girl, but not Heather. Afterwards I tried to retract. I mentioned you picking her up, then she wanted to know how you came to be out so late. So it all came out: how you were coming to Camlet because I'd phoned you, and Heather being missing, and her having told me that she went driving with Randal. Milly pushed me to find out how far it had gone and I tried to make light of it: a teenage crush, I said. She's going to speak to Randal. I feel awful, particularly with the police and everything.'

'But the police have nothing to do with your problem.'

'I know, but it was thoughtless of me. Coals of fire.'

'You were concerned about Heather, Milly must realize that.' On the other hand, he was thinking, each mother would be most concerned with her own offspring; Milly would be thinking: sex with a minor, a jail sentence.

Ruth said firmly, 'I'm going to have a proper talk with Heather. And this time I'm not going to be side-tracked by accusations of smothering or hysteria or prurience.'

'Prurience?'

'I'm supposed to be obsessed with rape, pregnancy, you name it. Well, I am! For God's sake, she's a child and he's a man!'

'Look, love, you can't –'

'I can! I'm her mother.'

'I was going to say that the way you're feeling, you'll only antagonize her.'

'You think you could do better?'

'Of course not –' He checked and thought about it. 'It might work,' he went on thoughtfully. 'Do you want me to? I'll have a shot if you're willing.'

'I'm a bad mother.' She slumped in her chair. 'My life revolves round her and she resents it. She's trying to get out from under me. I can understand that but it's too soon – at fifteen, too soon to – to be – and with a grown man.'

Prudently Charlie said nothing about the advantages of himself as a father-figure in a girl's life. He did say, 'You don't have to talk to her today, not about Randal. Milly may instil some reason into him. Why not wait until tomorrow at least? How would it be if I came up for supper this evening, would that make things a little less fraught for you?'

Chapter Three

The wind backed, the temperature climbed, and by the time Ruth came to leave Cougar a breeze was blowing soft and sticky from the south-west, sending the peat smoke whirling, ruffling the hens' feathers. Charlie stood at the gate, assessing the speed and direction of the clouds, considering the hazards of fast-melting snow. Living as he did now, close to the land, growing food, he'd acclimatized. 'Watch how you go,' he warned. 'There's ice under the snow. If it freezes tonight the roads will be skating rinks.'

'I shan't be out tonight, but you will.'

'I've got better tyres than you.' His thoughts flew to Heather, driving with Randal in his Mini Cooper, driving on ice. 'What are you having for supper?' he asked. 'Something we'll all like?' Meaning the kind of food that might keep Heather at home, not traipsing off to the village chippie, meeting Gow, even phoning him to pick her up at the road-end. 'Do your Spanish stew,' he urged. 'Buy some country wine and a couple of bottles of good claret. My treat.'

Ruth earned less in the winter when there were no holiday cottages to clean except at New Year, and she'd just lost a regular customer who'd gone into a home. As a consequence Charlie delighted in supplying her with small luxuries. Now he reflected that even braising beef was expensive but she'd never let him pay for meat, not as things stood anyway. He sighed as he watched her filthy Land Rover bucketing down the rutted road; she was a courageous lady, no doubt about that. His thoughts reverted to Randal, wondering whether Milly would find time to speak to her son today. Another only child, another mother – but different, he reminded himself with a start; Milly had Caspar. His father would be appalled when he discovered that Randal had any kind of relationship with a fifteen-year-old girl, and surely Caspar – a stupid fellow in Charlie's view – Caspar would think the worst? Charlie didn't; he thought Randal would be cautious in this respect, the man was a medical student, he'd practise safe sex. But then would he, with Heather? Oh my, he thought, is this how Ruth's mind is working? We've got a problem and no mistake.

Auchelie was little more than a large village that had grown up beyond the gates of the castle but it boasted a supermarket and a good butcher. Ruth winced at the price of claret but Charlie would do more than reimburse her. On her way out of the car park she glimpsed a green and white Mini Cooper in a corner, concluded that it was Randal's, and reflected that he was back from town early although Milly hadn't been specific. In this glen 'town' could mean any one of the larger places downriver, even Aberdeen. It was immaterial; Randal wasn't with Heather who was in school, and wouldn't be home till late afternoon when the bus dropped her at the road-end.

As she drove Ruth was wondering how long Charlie would put up with them – but he was fond of Heather, was even prepared to take her on as a stepdaughter. Was his affection for herself deep enough to absorb the child's hostility? She ruminated, driving slowly on an almost empty road, passing only the postie in his four-track, and Archy MacBean. Archy was employed at Blair as a kind of superior handyman, able to turn his hand to anything. Now he was trundling along on his quad bike, a bale of hay on the back, his collie between his knees, forepaws on the handlebars, startling in its appearance of control.

She came back to the middle of the road and her mind returned to her family. She admitted to herself that she was nervous when she visualized them living under one roof: Charlie, Heather, herself. Confrontations were disturbing enough now; in the presence of a third person they could be shattering. The chances of Charlie's being able to pour oil on such troubled waters seemed remote; she had visions of his giving up and walking away – and how guilty would they feel then? She because she had allowed him to join the family, Heather because she had driven her mother's friend away – my only friend, she thought with sudden surprise, for she was pessimistic concerning Milly's continued friendship. Wouldn't Randal blame everything on Heather? And there was bed, Ruth thought distractedly, sex bringing her back to Charlie. She had come to look on him as an affectionate relative: an uncle or an elder brother; she was uncertain about intimacy with him, mightn't Heather seize on such a close relationship as justification for an affair with Randal Gow?

The sun was westering as she rounded the last bend to see a stag high above her on the bank, antlers and coat gilded in the light. She touched her brakes carefully, knowing the tendency of deer and sheep to jump on to the road, but the beast turned and moved uphill, hinds scattering ahead of him. 'Nice,' she murmured, her mood lifted by the sighting. This was a good place to live – and perhaps everything would come right in the end. With both families, Charlie included, united to separate them, the youngsters couldn't hold out; after all, Randal had come straight home when he was – sent down – from Edinburgh. That indicated respect for his parents, and then she remembered that Randal was not a youngster, and that his home was the obvious place to go when in trouble: the living free and comfortable and with a mother who spoiled him rotten.

At four thirty she was dicing pineapple when she heard a

sound in the passage and opened the kitchen door to find Heather in the act of hanging up her jacket.

'I didn't hear the bus.' She was apologetic, as if she should have welcomed her daughter home at the front door like an illustration in a Victorian painting. Her glance went to the girl's feet: trainers. She wanted to shout: 'Get those wet things off this minute and find some dry socks!' She bit it back. Smothering: she mustn't smother. She became aware that Heather hadn't spoken, hadn't remarked on the smell that permeated the house. This was her daughter's favourite dish; with topside doused in Bulgarian red, simmering gently with onions and garlic and herbs, you could get drunk on the smell alone when Ruth did Spanish stew. This evening it excited no comment. Par for the course. After all, when did she last have a good word for her mother's cooking? Automatically Ruth pushed the kettle on the hob then took the initiative. 'Charlie's coming up,' she announced brightly, going to the cupboard for a mug, bringing milk and a tea bag to the table. She had a tumbler on the side, half-full of country wine. Still Heather said nothing. Ruth was suddenly alerted, thinking of illness. 'Are you feeling all right?'

'Of course!' Feigned surprise. 'Why shouldn't I be?'

'You're quiet.'

'What's there to say?' Another day that would have emerged with defiance, building to furious accusations of probing, of interference, of never allowing a person to lead her own life. Tonight the response was doleful.

'Aren't you hungry?' Anything to arouse some enthusiasm.

'No.'

Ruth exhaled. Something had happened at school. It would be revealed in time. She looked forward to Charlie's arrival; the man was a prop. She tossed back the rest of her wine and plunged, forgetting caution: 'Your feet are soaking. Go upstairs and run a bath.' Lacklustre eyes met hers and sheered away. 'Or if a bath is too much trouble' – she caught the acid note in her own voice – 'at least find some dry socks and your sheepie slippers. Next thing we know you'll be down with flu.'

The response was the faintest of shrugs, implying that flu was the least of one's problems.

Dear God, thought Ruth, pouring the last of the country red, eyeing the bottles of claret breathing on the counter, maybe it's more – comfortable – to have a son, I can't believe that Milly is going through this, that a man who's turned twenty hasn't outgrown childish sulks. Although, if Heather were coming down with something . . . She'd gone to her room. Castigating herself for stupidity Ruth dived for the drawer where she kept the thermometer and rushed upstairs. Heather was sitting on the edge of her bed and she turned to the door with a face so blank that Ruth was convinced she'd been staring at the wall.

'You didn't knock.' It was uttered without spirit. 'And no!' Her voice rising now. 'You're not putting that thing in my mouth!' She was actually cringing.

Ruth was shocked. 'Darling! A thermometer? For heaven's sake, what harm – is there something wrong with your mouth?'

'Don't be stupid. There's nothing wrong with me anywhere. I'm just fed up– I had a row – with Hayley Lamont. There. That satisfy you? Want to know what the row was about?' No longer apathetic, she was spitting like a cat, eyes blazing.

Ruth returned glower for glare. 'All right! If there's nothing wrong at least get those wet things off. And no, I don't want to know what you quarrelled about.' A lie, but to press the matter would precipitate more hostility, more delay before a change into dry clothes . . .

'Anyone at home?' came Charlie's voice from the foot of the stairs, and the front door closed. Ruth descended to find him hanging up his anorak. He followed her to the kitchen carrying a small rucksack. He sniffed happily, the sensitive mouth stretched in a froggy grin.

'Smells gorgeous.' He placed a bottle labelled Elderberry on the table and another: of The Macallan. 'You don't have to drink everything,' he murmured, eyeing the claret, handing her a banknote without embarrassment.

'I love you,' she said then, seeing his surprise, rolled her eyes towards the stairs. 'A bad mood. She says she quarrelled with Hayley. You're a breath of normality.' He nodded, unfazed. 'She'll be down,' she assured him, as if he were the one in need of reassurance.

He poured a little claret, tasted it and nodded again, fetching a clean glass for Ruth who had returned to the fruit salad. As she worked they discussed the deer, hoping that the animals would push back into the hills now that a thaw had set in. Ruth's fence wasn't really solid enough to deter hungry beasts and although she'd harvested all her sprouts, no one wanted deer to discover that a rickety fence was no obstacle to a vegetable plot

'Milly ought to have that garden refenced now,' Charlie said. 'Then your greens will be safe come next autumn.'

Ruth dropped the remains of the pineapple in the compost bucket. 'You think we'll still be here next autumn?'

'*Why not?*' It was an anguished cry from the doorway. Heather stood there, in trousers that bagged over her ankles and a Buckie sweater several sizes too large.

Ruth smiled. 'Well, you'll be warm enough' – carefully not asking where the strange jersey had come from, because it was a man's sweater and had surely been Randal's.

'You're planning to move again?' It was statement as much as question and it held a note of panic. Charlie studied the girl over the rim of his glass.

'No plans.' Ruth's voice was too steady. 'It's just that putting in a new deer fence seems rather committing, don't you think? How do we know where we'll be next September?'

'You're taking me out of school? *Again?* You can't *do* that!'

'You're quite right. You have to stay here another year at least. Anyway, even if we did move we wouldn't be leaving the locality, I promise.'

Ruth crossed to the refrigerator and only Charlie observed the girl's deep sigh, evidently of relief. Her face relaxed. 'You like that school,' he said, casual but warm.

'What?' She started as if she'd forgotten he was present. 'Yes. Yes, of course I do. I wouldn't be bothered about leaving any other school.'

There was a momentary silence, the adults knowing that it wasn't school that was so attractive. Ruth prodded the stew and wondered how Milly had fared with Randal. 'There was a break-in at Blair,' she said absently, adding mushrooms to a pan of sauté potatoes.

'A what?' Heather gaped at her mother's back.

'A burglary,' Charlie supplied. 'A painting's been stolen, and some ear-rings belonging to Mrs Gow.'

'Ear-rings?' She looked bewildered. 'Who broke in?'

'They've no idea.' Ruth had turned, her eyes going to Charlie. 'The police gave no indication. I mean' – she shrugged – 'they didn't say they'd be rounding up the usual suspects.'

'You were there?' Heather's question was more like an accusation. 'What were you doing at Blair?'

'Commiserating?' Ruth sounded uncertain.

'Oh, right.' She moved towards the door.

'I'm about to dish up,' Ruth warned.

'I'll be there.'

They listened to her on the stairs. 'Gone to phone Randal,' Ruth stated coldly. 'Wants to know what I said to Milly.'

They sat at the table, savouring the claret, waiting: as much for the food to cool a little as for Heather's return. She was back quite quickly and both adults had the same thought: Randal had switched off his mobile or he was engaged with Milly, or both.

After supper Heather excused herself with suspect politeness, cited homework, and went to her room. Ruth and Charlie washed up and then settled in easy chairs on either side of the stove. Conversation was a little stilted, both thinking of Heather and the Gows but tacitly avoiding the subjects. They dwelt with some deliberation on their gardens, wondering if, with global warming, they might experiment with species more usually confined to the milder south. They discussed greenhouses. At ten o'clock Ruth went to the bathroom, saying she'd look in on Heather to ask if she'd like a cup of cocoa before bed.

Left alone Charlie leaned back in his chair and contemplated the big wicker basket full of peats. Archy MacBean kept her supplied with the fuel in return for her occasional services as a cleaner. The man was a bachelor, a simple fellow who kept his house clean enough but he seemed to have taken a shine to the Ogilvies and would have cut the peat for nothing had Ruth allowed it. A good man, Archy MacBean.

Upstairs the cistern flushed, a few moments passed, he heard her cross the landing, pause, race down the stairs – he rose, wide-eyed. The door flew open.

'Where is she?' Ruth shouted. 'She's gone!'

'How? She didn't come downstairs. A window? Yes, her bedroom's above the porch.'

They went upstairs. Sure enough, Heather's window was closed but unlatched. There were no books or papers on the table that served as her desk, she had never intended doing any homework. Charlie avoided Ruth's eye.

'Do we call Milly?' She was torn between rage and diffidence.

He shook his head but in doubt rather than denial.

'She's with him.' Ruth's anger gathered strength. 'She called him and he's picked her up.'

'You could call *her*.'

They went back to the kitchen and the telephone, but Heather appeared to have switched off her mobile. 'What do we do now?' Ruth was racked by emotion: furious, concerned, incredulous.

'We wait.' Charlie was taking pleasure, despite everything, in her use of the plural. 'You're not on your own, my dear; Caspar is going to come down on him like a ton of bricks.'

'He could be too late.'

'Rubbish! The boy's irresponsible but he's too sensible to go all the way. He's a good-looking charmer and he can have any girl he wants; he's certainly not going to risk his freedom – and his career – for an under-age child.'

'You really think that?'

'I'll hazard a guess that the infatuation's all on her side. If he has agreed to meet her this evening then it could well be to tell her it's the last time. Milly and Caspar will have issued an ultimatum.'

'That's if they've spoken to him.'

'Milly will be worried out of her mind. If she hasn't confronted him already, she will after tonight.' He was grim and it occurred to Ruth that he might well approach the Gows himself, even Randal.

In Blair's dining room Caspar stabbed viciously at the Stilton while continuing to fulminate on the subject of the stolen painting. The monologue flowed over Milly like a tide. She stared at a crumb of cork in the dregs of her wine. 'You're not listening to me!' Caspar protested. 'I asked: why wasn't it insured separately?'

She shook her head as if to rid herself physically of other problems. 'It didn't have enough value,' she said weakly.

'Of course it did! It was worth stealing. Even the workmen knew that.' He had reached the conclusion that men working on the cascade were responsible for the theft. 'They knew none of these were worth the risk.' His sweeping gesture took in the portraits on the panelled walls around them, pictures so dark that only pale faces showed in the gloom.

Milly didn't spare them a glance. 'I seem to remember a fellow from the insurance company didn't think any of our pictures would reach a thousand.'

'The William Morris tapestry did.'

'That was different. And we sold it.' There was just a hint of censure in the comment.

'Well, the money was needed elsewhere.' For the water works actually, and it was himself who had insisted on selling the wall hanging. 'We could have sold the Farquharson had we known,' he grumbled. His voice rose: 'And why didn't the insurers value it correctly?'

'I doubt if they went down that passage. No one would expect to find a good picture in the back quarters.'

'So why was it put there in the first place?'

'I assume because Daddy didn't like it. I never really looked at it myself until I took the photograph, and that was only because I thought it might be worth five hundred.'

'And what *is* it worth? Fifty thousand?'

Milly sighed. It had been a long day and she was exhausted. 'A thief couldn't sell it,' she pointed out. 'It would be recognized immediately.'

'Not if it's smuggled out of the country. Fifty K down the drain: think what we could have done with that.'

'Actually I'm thinking of my ear-rings; now they were beautiful.'

'But worth no more than five hundred tops.'

'Caspar! It's only money.' He goggled at her. 'They were unusual,' she said stoutly: 'Agates cut on the cross; you don't remember them.'

'They might be worth more than you think. No, my dear' – as she shifted impatiently – 'you don't give nearly enough thought to the practical running of this place. If you would only think –'

'I've been thinking about Randal.'

It stopped him in mid-flight and the sudden silence was charged with tension. Rage ebbed like blood from his face and for a moment he looked frightened before he glanced down and started to fidget with his knife.

'He was provoked,' Milly said flatly.

'Of course.' Another pause. Caspar looked up, pugnacious again. 'She's not going to press charges.'

'She can't. She's a prostitute.' His eyebrows shot up.

'Randy told me,' she informed him in the same dry tone.

'I know it wasn't rape. He told *me* that. He's been quite frank about it, you know. He regrets hitting her but it was only a slap, something to do with – er – payment, so you may be right and she was a prostitute. However, no gentleman hits a woman, whatever she is.'

'He says it was an accident.'

Caspar ignored that. 'His career isn't finished,' he stated, as if in argument. 'It'll blow over. Storm in a teacup. The authorities don't want a public scandal any more than we – than anyone else. It'll be hushed up now that the girl's been exposed for what she is. He regrets it deeply, you know: the distress it's caused us. I mean to say: August and Elizabeth coming; she couldn't be expected to meet a boy who's been sent down for a scandal involving a prostitute.'

Milly's eyelids drooped and lifted slowly. 'It could be worse.'

'The trouble is,' he rushed on, raising his chin, paying no attention to her, 'it's not just that he's attractive to the girls, they're also bewitched by this place. They see themselves as ladies in a great house. It happens with the young princes: honey pots for moths.'

Milly's lips twitched, but he had it right to some extent; if cash were short around Blair there was certainly a great deal of land and property, and Randal would inherit eventually. Moreover he was a beautiful young man, although far removed from royalty. His looks came from his father's side; Milly had no illusions about her own appearance, indeed she thought herself fortunate to have secured such an – appropriate – husband. He cut a dashing figure for a laird, he had given her a son in his own image – and Caspar adored the castle and the estate, the stalking (he was a fine marksman); you might have thought he'd been born to it, most people did. He was domineering but that didn't bother Milly because he was malleable and she was circumspect. She hadn't told him about Randal and Heather Ogilvie, and was thankful that she hadn't done so before she spoke to her son. With luck he need never know.

Ruth had hit the nail on the head when she said that the affair was no more than a schoolgirl crush. Randy had shown no surprise and was only a trifle embarrassed to be taken to task by his mother. He'd agreed that he'd been stupid to allow the situation to go so far, to give in to Heather's advances in the first place . . . 'But, my dear,' Milly had protested, 'didn't you see how dangerous it was? If she was making all the running, you should have been on your guard; after all, you've done some psychology –'

'Mum, I'm not a psychiatrist, and it was rather flattering. She acts much older than her age, and she's very pretty. I lost sight of her being fifteen; I mean, it was only once or twice that I took her driving and then I was trying to find a way to back off without hurting her feelings . . .'

He'd assured her that he would put an end to the relationship at once although, as he pointed out, he would have to be gentle, she was only a kid. But he would tell her that since everyone knew now, she'd have to see how embarrassing it would be for her to continue to plague him. There'd be some tears, he said wryly, but he'd manage. Milly assumed that he was doing just that at this moment; he had gone out after dinner, nodding reassurance at her, glancing doubtfully at Caspar. She'd shaken her head; she wasn't going to tell his father, the unspoken rider was that it would be too much after the Edinburgh episode. She hoped devoutly that this second affair had been nipped in the bud, as the other one had been firmly squashed. Randy was twenty-two: young and – not immature, but somewhat naive, unworldly, girls took advantage one way or another. Heather was dazzled by his looks no doubt, the Edinburgh slut would have been angling for a rich husband although, as a prostitute . . . Milly was rather confused about Edinburgh.

*   *   *

Heather came home to Camlet about eleven o'clock and went straight to her room without coming in to say goodnight. Ruth looked at Charlie, swallowed, and left the kitchen without a word.

Her daughter was pulling off her fleece. Ruth pushed the door to but didn't close it. She might have said something about the unorthodox exit but the girl's eyes were red and swollen and she looked limp, as if about to collapse.

'What happened?' Ruth picked up the fleece and crossed to the wardrobe.

'Why trouble to ask?' Heather spoke to her back. 'You had to go and interfere: you and her. Well, you won. He says he's not going to see me again.'

'He doesn't want to go to prison, love. His parents will have spelled it out for him.'

'We weren't doing anyone – any of *you* any harm.' Her voice gained strength. 'You can't bear to see anyone else happy, can you? You're old, you've forgotten what it's like to be young, if you ever knew. Charlie Innes is just for security, you think I don't know he supports you? Services rendered, isn't it? Did he put you up to this? You know why he'd like to move in? So he can get his dirty paws on *me*.'

Ruth had steeled herself. She said coolly, 'You've only got a few more years to go and then you can marry. Get your exams over and then you've got some qualifications under your belt –'

'In America girls marry at fifteen –'

'Not middle-class girls –'

'You're a *cleaner*, for God's sake!'

'You'd rather I was on benefit?'

'If I married I'd be rich.'

Ruth couldn't suppress an angry laugh. 'Heather! You'd marry for money? Where's the love in that?'

'I could support you instead of that leech downstairs.' She was beside herself, contradictions rife. Tears welled up but they were of rage, not grief. 'You poisoned all the love,' she shouted. 'All that's left is horror. You've ruined everything, you've destroyed both of us. How are you going to live with yourself after what you've done?'

Ruth had no idea how she could remain cool and steady in the face of this onslaught. 'What does Hayley say?' she asked out of her strange composure.

Heather gaped, staring with wet eyes, then she collected herself. 'She's on my side.'

'Naturally, you'd expect loyalty from a friend. Why don't you call her?'

'I could do that. In fact that's just what I'm going to do if I can have a little privacy in my own room.'

Ruth left, not daring to say goodnight, closing the door quietly. Charlie's eyes were avid as she entered the kitchen. She smiled bravely.

'Venomous as a cobra,' she announced. 'Which is good. I'd dreaded despair. Now she's phoning Hayley and it's to be hoped they'll talk until she's exhausted. I doubt that she quarrelled with Hayley, something else must be wrong.'

'You're ahead of me. Was she with Randal?'

'What? Oh, of course, and he broke it off.' Ruth collapsed in her chair and recounted the conversation, omitting the references to himself, taking sips of the whisky he had poured for her. At the end she sighed and regarded him affectionately. 'You kept me sane tonight. If you hadn't been here I'd have been a total wreck by the time she came home. In fact, I'd probably have tried to stop her going out in the first place. Imagine trying to do that by force.' She shuddered.

There was a long silence which she broke. 'Now what are you thinking?'

'You want a distillation? Marry me.'

Her face lit up and she nodded some kind of acquiescence. 'I think I'm going to do just that – only let's get this little problem settled first –'

'It's settled, my love.' But even as he spoke the thought crossed his mind that she had only Heather's account of what had happened this evening. The solution seemed to have come too easily: that Milly should have issued an ultimatum, that Randal had accepted it, had said goodbye to Heather, and that the girl, after a predictable attack on her mother, was about to become a well-adjusted schoolgirl again.

Chapter Four

Ruth woke to the spring song of a blackbird; the sun had not yet risen and the sky was washed with the palest jade, clouds like blanket fluff fringed with pink. She surfaced with a weight on her mind, a legacy from past days, then she remembered that the worst problem had been resolved but relief didn't follow as it should. She was anticipating fallout, such as the need to decide on her attitude if Heather refused to go to school. Perhaps that curious fortitude would come to her aid as it had last night in the face of hysteria. She dressed, glancing out of the window now and again, trying to recoup her strength, suspecting that extreme fortitude arrived only in extreme situations, praying that there'd be no hostility at breakfast, knowing she couldn't rise to it twice in twelve hours.

Heather came downstairs ready for school, wearing uniform and carrying her sports bag, her hair combed, murmuring some acknowledgement to her mother's greeting. She ate a slice of toast, ignored the boiled egg keeping warm under its cosy but drank tea greedily. 'You look awful,' she said.

'I'm hung over.' Appreciating that her daughter could be concerned about her well-being, Ruth forbore to point out that the stress of waiting for her to come home last evening had called for strong drink.

'I'll be home on the bus,' Heather muttered, jumping up and snatching at her bag in passing.

Why the announcement? She always came home on the bus. The outer door slammed and Ruth slipped into the parlour to see her daughter pause at the garden gate. Evidently deciding that the remaining snow was too slushy for her bike she started down the track on foot. Relieved to see that she was wearing her wellies Ruth returned to the kitchen, ate the egg and toast and, leaving the washing-up for the afternoon, drove to Archy MacBean's cottage.

The man was an early riser and had gone to work by the time she arrived. His two cats were crouched at the door, rising in unison to weave about her ankles as she retrieved the key from under a flower pot and let herself inside.

Since Archy was a reasonable housekeeper she'd become adroit at finding jobs that needed her attention and today she started on the brass. Archy's father had been the horseman at the castle and the parlour walls shone with the beautiful brasses that had graced the breast straps of Shires and Percherons, animals immortalized in foggy photographs. After the brasses she worked in the bathroom and kitchen, using a toothbrush on those awkward places that a man missed, attacking peaty stains with steel wool. She was scrubbing underneath the kitchen taps when she heard an engine outside.

'Forgotten something?' she asked brightly as Archy entered.

'You've not heard?'

'Heard what? Who – has something happened?' Her thoughts flew to Heather and the school bus. She clutched at the sink for support.

'Don't take on.' He was concerned. 'It's no one we know; it's that Cummings, a fellow on the water works.'

'Oh, one of Blair's workers.' She released her grip on the sink. 'What happened to him?'

'He must have been drunk. They found him on the back road. He'd have been walking home from the village to the camp.'

'And? What happened? He collapsed – or –'

'That's right. He'll have collapsed and then he died. A stroke, that's what it was.'

'How sad.' It was automatic and she performed a double-take. 'But he'd be young for a stroke, surely: a labourer. How old was he?'

'All that gang's in their twenties but age makes no difference when they drink and smoke like chimneys.' Archy did neither on the grounds that the first robbed a man of his self-control and the other made him smell bad. He had seen bottles at Camlet but he made allowances for Ruth – and she didn't smoke.

'So what's brought you home in the middle of the morning?' she asked.

'I was passing. Lamont's laid up with the flu and I was in the Easter Wood seeing after the pheasants. I'm on my way to the sheep now.' Lamont was the gamekeeper.

She made coffee, thinking he'd called in for a gossip; this house wasn't on the way from Easter to Blair. 'I'm going to ask Mrs Gow if you can fence my garden,' she told him. 'The deer will be in next winter otherwise.'

'Sure. I'll do that once the evenings start to draw out.'

'Wait for the go-ahead from Mrs Gow. She has to pay for it.'

'I'll not want paying.'

'No, Archy, that's not how it's done.' Damn, she shouldn't have mentioned it. 'Mrs Gow would want to arrange things.'

'She can't say anything if I'm doing it in my own time.'

She gave up; this man was as stubborn as a mule. Anyway, she thought, smiling, I could be married and living at Cougar by the time the evenings get longer.

'Something funny?' he asked, smiling with her. He really was a sweet guy. Charlie called him a holy fool.

'What do you think of Charlie Innes?' It wasn't flippant; she was interested in his opinion, and he would think nothing unusual to the question.

'I think you should marry him.'

She gasped. 'He's a steady man,' he assured her. 'I don't *know* mind, but I reckon he'll make a good father for Heather.'

'You're a very perceptive fellow, Archy MacBean.'

'You asked me. Now, I've been long enough gossiping. I've got all me sheeps to feed, and the lambing ewes to look at. Tell Heather I've not forgotten.'

'Forgotten what?'

'Why, the first lamb. I promised I'd let her know. She wants to see it. But it'll be a while yet, thank the Lord. This thaw isn't the end of winter; come March we'll have another heavy fall. We always do.'

She left soon after him, putting the cats out, locking up, replacing the key. She drove to the village for bread and milk. In the wide space outside the high gates of Blair two vehicles were stationary: a police car and a white Audi. A group of men, two in uniform, a couple in plain clothes, stood beside the cars deep in conversation. She guessed that these last were the detectives on the trail of the stolen painting, but at the bakery customers and assistants were buzzing with speculation concerning Blair's workman, implying the CID was looking into his death. Apparently the man had not been found dead on the road at all; one of his mates, coming home late, had discovered him alive and taken him back to the camp where the men lived in caravans. He had died in the night.

Ruth absorbed this without comment, thinking that there were bits missing; people were exchanging significant glances but she was well aware that in a glen where nothing happened more exciting than a car crash or a walker missing in the hills, any hint of suspicion concerning a death is seized on with ghoulish delight.

Back at home she called Charlie. He hadn't left Cougar this morning and he listened to her news without interruption. 'What do you think?' she asked.

'It looks a bit awkward for the chap who's supposed to have found him collapsed on the road.'

'Supposed?'

'Well, he could have run him over, couldn't he? Was he drunk too?'

* * *

In the interview room at Auchelie's police station a massive man by the name of Dougal MacPherson faced two detectives across a table. They had introduced themselves as Detective Sergeant Hay and Detective Constable Skene and they were polite and pleasant – so far – and had sympathized with him over the death of his mate.

'Of course you wouldn't remember much' – Skene was indulgent – 'you'd been drinking . . .'

'I wasn't drunk.' MacPherson was belligerent. 'I told you: I'd had a couple of whiskies and beer, and that was it.'

'The roads were very bad,' mused Hay.

'Ay, but I didna touch him. You always go slow on that road because of the deer. Kill one of the man's beasts and I'd be out of a job, wouldn't I? I saw Jimmie miles ahead in me headlights and had plenty of time to stop without skidding.'

'You could have killed him,' Hay said.

MacPherson was terrified. His eyes bulged, his mouth hung open. He was no charmer at the best of times: dull red hair already thinning, watery eyes, much of his substance fat. 'I want –' he gasped, and stopped.

Hay, himself corpulent, but smooth, sporting a silk tie, raised expressive eyebrows. 'You want what?'

'If you're accusing me you gotta charge me. I want my solicitor.'

'What am I accusing you of?'

'M— You said as I killed him.'

'I said you could have killed him. You should never move a man who's unconscious, you know that.' Gently reproving.

'He weren't unconscious, just drunk. He'd passed out.' The police waited. 'So I put him in the car and took him back to the camp and put him on his bed. You know all this. He was alive!'

'What we're saying is you could have done the damage just by moving him.'

MacPherson blinked, his slow brain considering the suggestion, wondering if it were an accusation or an escape route. He licked his dry lips. 'I wasn't to know. You reckon I done wrong to move him? I only did what I thought was right – it wasn't the first time by a long chalk: take a mate home, let him sleep it off. He'd had a skinful.'

'You had words in the bar.' Not a question but a shot in the dark. He'd told them already that he'd been drinking with the dead man during the evening and now Hay pondered that fact, speaking a thought aloud.

He'd hit pay dirt. 'It were nothing!' MacPherson blustered quickly. 'He wanted a bottle to take home and he were skint, and drunk already. No way was I going to buy a bottle. That's all there was to it.'

The detectives exchanged glances. 'We'll check it,' Skene said.

The man's jaw dropped and snapped shut. 'They threw him out,' he admitted. 'He tried to get a bottle on tick and when the woman refused he said something as he shouldn't, and she told me to take him home.' A pause. He knew he had to end it. 'And he wouldna get in the car, said he'd make his own way back.' He sat and glowered at them, determined not to continue. He was huge and Cummings had been wiry but small. Had there been a fight? They guessed he didn't know his own strength.

'And?' Skene pressed.

'Nothing.'

'You followed close behind.'

'I never! Nowhere near. I stayed in town.'

'Where?'

'At The Shieling. You can ask them. They'll remember me, there wasn't many customers. I were there at least an hour.'

Skene's lips stretched in the ghost of a grin. Hay nodded. 'You had a bit more than two whiskies and chasers then.'

'So? I wanted to give Jimmie the chance to get to bed. I'd had enough aggro for one night.'

There was a knock at the door. Skene stood up and went out leaving Hay and MacPherson regarding each other, the one thinking that this fellow would break quite easily now, wondering whether it had been an accident or a deliberate running down; MacPherson sweating copiously, waiting to be charged with murder.

Skene opened the door, signalled to his superior, and resumed his seat. Hay found Tom Malcolm outside: the uniformed sergeant who had responded to Blair's call about the burglary. 'We've had the doctor on the phone,' he said. 'Cummings was struck by a motor: right leg broke to bits, only his trousers holding it together.'

Hay nodded his satisfaction. 'And we've got the driver in there.' Gesturing to the room behind him. 'Marks on the trousers?'

'Ay, paint marks sure enough: green.'

'What colour car does MacPherson drive?'

Malcolm didn't know. Hay returned to the room. In the depths of despair MacPherson watched him take his place and waited for the caution. He responded automatically when asked for the registration number of his car.

'Make? Colour?' Hay asked quietly.

It was a Toyota and it was red.

They would check of course, but Hay knew that however drunk this fellow had been, even so drunk he hadn't realized that the man he carried to the camp was dead, he hadn't been the driver who'd run him down.

'We've got a hit-and-run here,' Hay said. 'Land Rovers are green, more's the pity. On the other hand there wouldn't be many of 'em on that road last night.'

They were eating roast beef sandwiches in The Shieling, a quiet bar in the main street. They'd checked MacPherson's story with the licensee's wife, and it was she who had been behind the bar last evening. He'd had a deal to drink, she said, but he'd been amenable and had found his way out without blundering into the furniture.

'If he didn't do it, why did he lie?' Skene asked.

'He'd have been well over the limit,' Hay reminded him.

'He'd been drinking for at least three hours.' They'd visited The Claymore where the two men had been drinking earlier and learned that throughout the evening they'd been on whisky with beer chasers. 'They were both plastered,' Hay went on, 'and our man was driving. He'd be afraid of losing his licence – and then the way things were going he'd be suspected of running his mate down. Now I wonder . . . Was Jimmie Cummings dead or alive when he was found?'

'It doesn't make any difference to MacPherson. He didn't do it; that is, Jimmie wasn't hit by Mac's car. And Mac was drunk enough that he could have thought the man had just passed out, as he told us. So he shoved him in the passenger seat, or in the back, never noticed his leg in the dark; anyway, he'd expect the guy to be limp.'

'But if Jimmie was alive he might have said something, like who hit him, or rather, what. We'll need to go back, persuade Mac to talk.' Hay smiled evilly. 'Point out that he was way over the limit: drunk driving.'

'There's no proof now.'

'Oh, I think we can make Mac see it's in his best interests to co-operate. Meanwhile if we can get Forensics to give us an opinion on that green paint – just a visual assessment, the technical report's going to take an age – then we'll know what shade of green belongs to the killer's car.'

Archy MacBean met Charlie on the road to Cougar. Archy pulled his quad off the track and came to the Range Rover's window. 'I been seeing to the hoggs,' he said, aware that it was only courteous to explain his presence on a private road, even if it provided easement to Blair's hill grazing.

'You've still got sheep up there?' Charlie was surprised; young fattening hoggs were brought down for the winter.

'There's always some left behind after gathering.' Archy had his blind spots and suffered from the delusion common to hillmen that no townie could become knowledgeable on rural matters however long he lived here.

Charlie saw that sheep were only a gambit; Archy had an ulterior motive for stopping by. 'We have some spare eggs,' he said. 'Would you like half a dozen?'

'I'm all right for eggs, thanks.' Archy looked down the pasture, no longer snow-covered but striated with plump wet drifts. 'Take a while for this lot to drain,' he observed. 'Are you keeping dry?' He nodded towards Cougar.

'I'm fine.' Charlie had spent money on damp-proofing. 'Ruth has the odd leak here and there.'

'Oh dear.' Archy was concerned. 'She was saying only this morning that she needed her garden fencing. I never thought to ask about the roof.'

'Of course, she comes to you today.' Charlie's eyes glazed as he wondered why the man hadn't been at work when Ruth was cleaning his house.

'I looked in,' Archy said quickly. 'I'd been up to the birds in Easter Wood. Lamont's down with the flu. I was telling her the news.'

'Ah, yes. She called me. I don't think I ever met Cummings. I suppose he was drunk?'

'It was a hit-and-run.' Archy was indignant. 'What sort of a man does that: kills another human being and doesn't stop? Why, you'd go back for a deer to make sure it was dead.'

'You're saying this fellow was run down and the driver didn't stop?'

Archy didn't hear it as a question. 'And there's green paint on his clothes.' His eyes were steady on Charlie.

'Green.' Charlie stared at the Range Rover's navy-blue bonnet.

'The police is checking all green motors,' Archy said, unblinking.

'That will include most Land Rovers. But one of them will be marked, dented; even a headlight smashed possibly.'

'You're all right.' Archy smiled.

'I know.' Charlie's antennae were bristling. 'What time did it happen?'

'That I don't know but it would be late on. He'd been drinking much of the evening so it would be around ten or eleven.'

'I was with Ruth – and Heather – at Camlet.' Charlie suppressed a smile, seeing that this put Ruth in the clear.

'Her 'Rover's clean,' Archy said, as if gifted with telepathy. 'I mean, it's dirty but there's no new dents on it.'

Charlie did smile at that. 'You looked!'

'Of course.'

The smile died. So the motive for this visit was revealed: Archy was making it his business to reassure his friends that Ruth was not a suspect in a hit-and-run fatality.

'It's serious, isn't it, Archy?'

'A man was killed.' It was a rebuke. 'They're looking at everyone with a green motor.'

'I heard you the first time. So who could that be?'

'All the old Land Rovers of course, but otherwise it's not a popular colour. Green's unlucky. The only car that comes to mind is young Randal's Mini.' Charlie's eyes wandered. 'You'll want to be away home now,' Archy directed. 'Get your hens shut up before that old fox comes visiting. I seen tracks up back of your place.'

'Mrs Gow's away to town,' Isabel Lamont told Sergeant Malcolm, 'but himself is about. Mr Randal? I've not seen him all day. Cars? They must have – what? Five, six? There's the Bentley, two Land Rovers, the Range Rover, the Subaru – why d'you want to know all this? *Colour?* Look, their cars is no concern of mine, I'm just the housekeeper. You want to know the colours of their cars, Tom Malcolm, you go and ask himself. You should know anyway; you're supposed to know what's what.' Flushed, she bustled round the kitchen table and Malcolm stepped out of her way sharply.

'Just routine inquiries,' he soothed. 'We're asking everyone. Where is Gow?'

'*Mister* Gow is probably in the stables. We're short-handed and we're busy. This isn't Balmoral, you know; at Blair we all muck in, and Mr Gow will be his own groom today, Lamont laid up and all, MacBean doing two men's work.'

'The stables,' Malcolm said heavily. 'That'll be down the passage where the painting was hung, right? The one that was stolen.'

Isabel swelled with contempt. 'Don't you look at me! You think I snuck in and carried off that great old-fashioned thing?'

'Did you?'

She snorted and turned to her stove, not deigning to answer.

Malcolm found Caspar in the stables across the yard brushing a tall bay gelding. 'Any progress?' he barked as the sergeant's bulk cut off the light from the doorway.

'It's early days, sir. We're going door to door; they've drafted in extra men.'

'You reckon someone's going to come out and admit it, just like that?'

'We can check. We're asking for make and colour. They know they have to tell the truth, all details are on computer.'

Caspar was immobile, staring at him, brush and curry comb poised in mid-air. 'Colour and make?' His voice climbed.

'Of their cars.'

'What the devil's that got to do with my Farquharson?'

Mrs Gow's actually, Malcolm thought. 'I'm talking about the fatal accident, sir.'

'Ah. Yes. Of course.' Absently Caspar flicked at the glossy withers. 'Colour and make, eh? You've got a witness then?'

'As good as. We've got a paint sample from the victim's clothes.'

A pause. 'Is that so? That's good. Good. So you can identify the vehicle involved?'

'We can identify the paint.'

Caspar came out from the stall, cleaning the brush. He took a comb from the window sill and moved to the gelding's head. He said delicately, as if talking to the animal: 'Are you going to tell me whose car it was? Or should I not be asking that kind of question?'

'It was green,' Malcolm said. 'Racing green, which cuts out all the Land Rovers.'

'That's a relief.' Caspar didn't elaborate. It was unnecessary; he'd know that Malcolm was familiar with Blair's vehicles.

'Your son has a green Mini,' the sergeant said.

'That's right, but a motor that hit a man will be marked. His isn't.' Malcolm didn't speak. The horse shifted a foot. 'Go and look yourself,' Caspar said.

Malcolm drew back and glanced round the yard. A drab green Land Rover stood on the cobbles and the rear of a grey Bentley showed through the arched doorway of what would have been a coach house.

'I don't see a Mini,' Malcolm said.

'He must be out then. He'll be back in time for dinner. I'll tell him to run down to the station, shall I?' The tone was patronizing: the laird humouring the peasantry.

'I'd appreciate that: just as a matter of elimination.'

'Meanwhile' – Caspar was incensed that the fellow didn't know his place – 'what's happening about the Farquharson?'

Malcolm hesitated as he'd been about to leave. He turned back. 'You reckon the two crimes are connected?'

Caspar stopped combing the mane and put one hand on the horse's shoulder. The whites of his eyes showed in the dim light. 'Connected?' he breathed. 'That's not possible – I mean, how could they be? Or are you thinking that one of the workmen . . . like, er, thieves falling out?'

'You suspected the workmen, sir.'

'True, true. It was his friend who found the dead man, wasn't it? MacPherson.'

'We've had him down at the station, helping us with our inquiries.' Malcolm was expressionless. 'He drives a red car. But we have another possibility; Cummings might have been alive when MacPherson found him, in which case he could have said who ran him down.'

'MacPherson hasn't said?'

'Someone's up there now, asking more questions. I'll be back at the station by six if your son cares to drop in, just to keep the record straight.'

Malcolm left and shortly afterwards Milly drove into the yard in her Subaru. Caspar emerged from the stable as she opened the boot to reveal the shopping. 'I'll give you a hand with that.'

'I passed Malcolm at the gate. Is there any news?'

He threw a glance at the kitchen door. 'He didn't come about the painting, and I'd rather not stand about gossiping.'

'The village is doing nothing else.' The tone was dry. She pulled bags towards her. 'They're saying Cummings was run down by someone in a green vehicle, so they're questioning everyone who owns an old Land Rover.'

'Actually Malcolm mentioned Randy.'

'He would. No one's exempt.'

'But Randy's in the clear. There won't be a mark on his Mini.'

'Caspar! As if!'

He spread his hands. 'It's impossible, bizarre! How could anyone knock a man down and not know it? Why, you feel the impact if you hit a rabbit. No way could Randy have struck a man and not known. He'd have seen him in the headlights first anyway.'

'There's no need to work yourself into a tizzy, dear.' She was soothing, not looking at him.

'Well, Malcolm pointing out that our son has a green car! Naturally I was incensed.'

'He was only doing his job. I hope he apologized when

he saw the car. Are you going to help me get this stuff inside or do I have to do it myself?'

Absently Caspar reached for the bags. His wife was looking round the yard. 'Where *is* Randy?'

'He's not home yet.' Loaded, Caspar started for the kitchen door.

'He'll be back for dinner.' Milly slammed the boot with an air of finality.

Chapter Five

Camlet was the last inhabited house in the glen so, after dropping Heather, the school bus turned round at the foot of the track and returned to Auchelie. Mindful of road conditions (although the plough had come through and cleared the last of the slush) Ruth waited until five o'clock before calling the driver in the village. He was home and no, he hadn't come as far as Camlet simply because he'd dropped Heather at Hayley's place. Furious, Ruth telephoned the Lamonts who lived in the lodge at the entrance to Blair. Annoyed and barely polite, Isabel said she would go upstairs and tell Heather immediately.

Using her mobile Heather called home and apologized. She'd meant to phone before but they'd got talking and anyway it was only five o'clock and her mother knew where she was – 'I didn't!' Ruth cried. 'You could have been – there could have been an accident! I had to call Billy to find out what had happened.' Billy was the bus driver. 'I'll be there right away,' she grated, and dropped the phone in the face of Heather's protests.

Walking into the Lamont kitchen she apologized brusquely but remembered to ask after Lamont. She had her hands full, Isabel grumbled, what with himself taking to his bed, and all the trouble up at the castle, police in and out, Gow walking round like a death's head, the mistress snapping and carping, and that boy leaving his room in a right mess; glad to see the back of him at last, she was.

'Randal's gone back to university?' Ruth felt such a rush

of relief that it must have shown in her face because Isabel's eyes sharpened.

'I'll give the girls a shout,' she said, and went to call from the foot of the stairs. 'Unusual for them,' she murmured, coming back. 'Most often they're playing music loud enough to damage a soul's eardrums. Hayley has to be thinking of her dad for a change.'

More likely they had too much to talk about, Ruth thought grimly, wishing she could be a party to Heather's confidences, wondering, as ever, where she'd gone wrong. Even Hayley, entering the kitchen behind her friend – a plain girl in granny glasses which did nothing for the prim features she'd inherited from her mother – even Hayley looked hostile. Ruth saw the image she must present: the repressive, obsessive mother who couldn't let her daughter visit her friend for an hour without climbing the wall.

Heather didn't speak on the way home. Ruth said it was a relief to have the roads clear at last, soon they'd be seeing lambs, that there was a fine show of snowdrops this year. The girl responded with grunts before lapsing into silence.

Over supper Ruth made no further attempts at conversation, her daughter toying with her lemony chicken and appearing dejected rather than sulky. Afterwards, washing up, Ruth wondered aloud about homework. She couldn't be bothered, Heather said. Ruth studied the other's face. 'Are you feeling all right?'

Heather opened her mouth – a quick rebuff? – and checked. She dried a plate carefully. 'Not really.'

'Where do you feel it?'

'It's something I ate. No, no' – as her mother's eyes flew to the basin containing the rest of the chicken – 'lunchtime, I mean.'

'You took a sandwich. What was in it?'

'I swapped it for some *koftas*.'

'You went – oh, the girl from the Indian restaurant. You think the meat was off?'

'No, Mum, honest. They tasted lovely. Too rich maybe. I'm not used to them.'

Ruth's eyes narrowed as she turned back to the sink. Heather and her friends were always swapping their sandwiches for exotic Indian snacks. No one ever suffered yet. This wasn't food poisoning. 'Randal's gone back,' she observed, addressing a saucepan.

'Who said?' It was quick and heated.

'Mrs Lamont.'

'What else did she say?'

'Nothing.' Ruth knew what was implied. 'The police are in and out of Blair,' she conceded, keeping the conversation going.

'What for?'

'The stolen painting?' She heard her own query. 'And the hit-and-run – you heard about that? One of the men working on Caspar's cascade – oh, that's hilarious: Caspar's cas –' but Heather had gone, hand over mouth, snatching at the door, plunging upstairs. The bathroom door slammed. Ruth sighed and considered the saucepan; it couldn't be the *koftas*, they must have been eaten hours ago. The chicken then? But she'd eaten more than her share and there was nothing wrong with her. It had to be emotional stress; the child flipped after hearing that Randal had left. Well, if she had retained hopes that the affair – relationship, Ruth amended quickly – wasn't over, it was obvious that Randal had been scared off. And had left without any intimation to Heather, judging from her astonishment at the news. Poor child, she thought, remembering her own crushes at that age; she must try to think of something exciting to do this weekend.

Footsteps crossed from bathroom to bedroom. Ruth went to the foot of the stairs and heard the tell-tale squeaks of a mobile, then silence, then more dialling. She moved away. Randal had gone, she had no wish to hear her daughter pouring out her broken heart to Hayley. She wondered how, when Heather reappeared, the subject of Randal might be broached, whether it should be broached at all. She decided that, if comfort were needed, it would be asked for, one way or another.

Heather came down after half an hour. 'It had to be the *koftas*,' she said. 'But it hasn't put me off Indian food, it was just a one-off.'

'Tell me about it.' Ruth was effusive. 'I could just as well have bought something past its sell-by date.'

'That's what I told Hayley. I've been talking to her.'

'I'm sorry I had to come and pull you out of the Lamonts'.'

'That's all right, you had to come sometime.' Heather took a mug from the cupboard. 'What are you watching tonight?'

Ruth was sitting with a mug of tea and the *Radio Times*. 'There's nothing that interests me. You look.' She passed the magazine across the table. Heather sat down and opened it at random. 'I broke it off with Randal,' she said, extremely casual.

'Yes?' It was strangled. 'Last night?' Ruth added weakly, remembering that screaming tirade, the accusations.

'We were driving, and we stopped and talked it over.'

'Upsetting for you.'

'Not really. I mean, I controlled it until I was coming up the track. Then it hit me.'

So she took it out on her mother. 'I've been there,' Ruth said.

'Have you?' The astonishment sounded genuine. There was a pause. 'I'll be glad when we move,' Heather said.

'But – we wouldn't be going far. I did say: you'll stay at this school, there's no question of you being uprooted with exams in the offing.'

'I just want to get away from the pass.'

'The *pass*?' What the hell was this?

'Here – our pass.' Beyond Camlet the road started to climb to cross the watershed before descending towards Speyside. The high point was the Lairig Dhu, the black pass. 'We said goodbye at the foot of it.' Heather made it sound like a suicide pact. 'I never want to see that lay-by again.'

'How did Randal take it?'

Heather turned a page of the *Radio Times*. 'He was devastated.'

'It would have been difficult – living next door as it were.'

Her daughter looked up sharply. 'What would have been difficult?'

'Not seeing each other.' Ruth felt as if she were walking on eggs.

'We discussed it. He said he had to go away. We didn't stay there long – it was cold. He brought me home and went straight back to the castle.' Heather held her eye. 'His mother was waiting for him.'

Ruth tried not to show her confusion. She could think of nothing to say but she felt as if something were expected of her. 'So that's it,' she said, adding desperately, 'What would you like to do this weekend?'

Now the girl looked lost, as if at an unexpected reaction, but she rallied quickly. 'There's a concert in Cromack; we could go to that: Hayley and me. If you take us to Auchelie we can catch the bus.'

Ruth didn't offer to take them all the way to town, knowing they'd prefer to be alone. 'So long as you take your mobile,' she said unhappily, disappointed that they wouldn't be doing something together, glad Charlie had talked her into buying the mobile which her daughter used most extravagantly for chatting – and that she tolerated in view of those occasions when the phone was used for emergencies, like missing the last bus.

'I always take my mobile,' Heather said loftily – which was nice, indicative of a return to the adolescent. A return from what? Ruth blocked out that thought.

DS Gordon Hay was married to a plump and active Aberdonian who, once the children were grown and had flown the coop, had taken up Art. She wasn't much good at it but she found it most enjoyable, which was the main thing, and she was knowledgeable. She had dabbled in water colours, now she was into oil painting.

When Hay came home after checking reports on green motors in Glen Essan Catrin was watching a documentary on Joseph Farquharson. 'Not very informative,' she told him, turning off the sound, rising to go to the kitchen and take his supper out of the oven. He was a considerate husband, usually phoned half an hour or so before he expected to be home.

'I should have watched that,' he mused, washing his hands at the sink. 'It was a Farquharson painting that was stolen from Blair Essan.'

'But you're not working on that.'

'No.' He hesitated. 'Not really. I'm on the hit-and-run up there; same village though. A coincidence – of course.' He spoke slowly, the tap running.

'Turn that tap off, man! All my hot water going down the drain!' Hay reached for the towel. She eyed him shrewdly from behind the new glasses that made her look like Mrs Bun the baker's wife. 'Not a coincidence?' she ventured.

'You see' – staring blankly at the salmon pie, making no comment, and he loved salmon – 'Gow suspects his own workmen as having stolen the painting, and it's one of them has been killed.'

'What – murder?'

'I didn't say that.' He pulled out his captain's chair, his movements automatic, his mind back in Auchelie. 'He was killed, yes; I needled his mate, suggested he could have done it: driving home drunk and the roads icy – but murder?' He looked up at her. He'd known her hit the nail on its head more than once in their twenty-five years of marriage. 'Why? How would it tie in? Of course, the painting could be worth a tidy sum.'

'What is it?'

'How do I know, woman? I never saw it. The uniformed

man says it was a big old-fashioned thing; he's seen a Polaroid: just snow and a wood and some rabbits, he says.'

'Help yourself, do.' She nudged the pie dish towards him but she wasn't thinking of food. She strained the broccoli and served him from the pan. 'It sounds like *Afterglow*,' she said, 'but –'

'That's right, that was the title someone used.'

'It's not the original then; that's in the city Art Gallery. It's either a print or . . .' She frowned.

'No!' He grinned. 'You're saying it's a fake?'

'Forgery?' she murmured. 'But Joseph painted the same subject several times . . . Is it signed?'

'Catrin, this is not my case! All the same, it's odd; it'll bear looking into. I'll speak to young Fleming tomorrow; he's working on it.' He regarded his plate without seeing it. 'Now, if it was a fake, could that have any bearing on Cummings' death?'

Catrin decanted a McEwan's Export into his tankard. 'Eat while it's hot,' she ordered, and stood back. 'Isn't there some sign as to what hit him?'

'Green paint.' He nodded, his fork poised. 'And it's racing green. There's a green Mini Cooper I want to look at tomorrow. The owner wasn't around this afternoon. He's supposed to be looking in at Auchelie this evening.'

'Who is it?'

'Young Randal Gow of all people! And I'm not sure that he hasn't been up to something dodgy at his university. He came home a week or so after New Year. Now why would a man in his fourth year at medical school stay home for two months, eh?'

At Blair Caspar and Milly were drawn with worry. Randal's place at the table was set but empty. Neither of his parents had eaten much, Milly had sipped a little burgundy, Caspar was on his third large whisky. 'They're going to find out,' he said dully.

Her face set. 'There's nothing to find out. And now he's gone back, that shows he has nothing to be afraid of. What I can't understand is why you couldn't tell me that he'd gone to Edinburgh.'

'I – wasn't sure. I just assume he has.'

'But why should you assume it if he didn't say so himself?'

He sighed and muttered something. 'What was that?' She was fierce, certain that he was keeping something from her.

'I said it looks bad.' She inhaled sharply. 'I mean,' he went on quickly, shifting before her stare, 'Malcolm's expecting him to call at the station. I said he'd be back.'

'And you knew he wouldn't be.' Her voice dropped dangerously. 'And how are you going to explain to Malcolm tomorrow? Why didn't you tell him the boy's gone back to university?'

'Because – because I wanted Malcolm to think Randy was in the area, knocking around somewhere. I couldn't have him thinking the boy had disappeared.'

'*He hasn't disappeared!* And there's nothing wrong with his car, he wasn't on that road last night!' She was almost shouting – which she could do with impunity, none of the staff lived in. 'He just isn't answering his mobile. Did you try his flat? No. Then I'm going to.'

DS Fleming was tail-end dog next morning, driving up the glen with DC Grant. Hay and Skene were ahead in the white Audi, its status somewhat marred by its M registration, Fleming thought sourly. He was a youngster on the fast track and he ran an old Alfa which had cost him seven thousand six months ago and whose repair bills were increasing his overdraft alarmingly. In fact it was in the garage now and he was in Grant's Cavalier, dreaming of a 3-litre Alfa at 25K on offer in the local paper and – not unconnected – how he might tie in his own case with that of Hay, thus earning promotion. Fleming did Art but only by default, and he had with him the Polaroid of the stolen Farquharson. The photograph had come back this morning from experts at the Art Gallery, along with other prints.

The police assembled at the station in Auchelie where Malcolm was waiting for them. Hay's first question concerned young Gow's Mini. Was it marked? 'He didn't come home,' Malcolm said. There was a pregnant silence.

'What's his father got to say about that?'

'I talked to Mrs Gow.' Malcolm was cool, he'd done his part. 'She said her son had returned to his university and she gave me the numbers of his mobile and the fixed line in his flat. There was no reply from that, and he's not answering to his mobile.' He'd made no attempt to contact the man this morning, leaving that to the detectives. Yes, he said in answer to Hay's next query, MacPherson had stuck more or less to his story that Cummings was unconscious when he found the man, but now he admitted that he could have been dead, there was no way of telling. Meaning he was too drunk to tell the difference, was Hay's comment, not that much concerned because by now everyone knew that a dying declaration would have been superfluous; the paint on Jimmie's clothes was surely racing green and Hay was looking for a Mini Cooper.

They left Malcolm at the station and drove to the castle, each team knowing that both cases had taken significant leaps forward, each aware that there could well be a connection, but both Hay and Fleming, experts at compartmentalizing, following different threads, the one concentrating on the driver and his Mini, the other on footprints in the snow.

'What my boy's done,' Caspar said loudly, after they'd found him in a dungeon referred to as the gun-room, 'he's gone out and left his mobile in the flat, switched on. He's always doing that. His mother can't contact him either. She needs to get in touch with him about a party next month. He went off without discussing it.'

'You'll be worried,' Hay said, a note of concern there: father to father.

'No. Why?' It was a bark.

'He left here, he hasn't turned up at his destination. Where is he?'

'How should I know? It's his life!' Caspar had his back to the light from a barred lancet window, but they didn't have to see the man's face to know that he must be flushed. Hay looked at Skene. They were seated on one side of a wide desk, the intention surely to keep them in their place – junior non-coms up before the commanding officer – but roles were reversed and it was Caspar who was presenting as the unhappy interviewee.

Skene said gently, 'You didn't think in terms of an accident, sir?'

The man jerked to attention. 'He's an excellent driver!' He back-tracked a pace in order to preserve the image of a macho son: 'Too fast – sometimes – but always in control, you know, knows his limits. Good little car too.' His form loomed, seeming to swell with indignation at the implied slur on his son's expertise. 'His mother's anxious,' he admitted, 'but women . . . Only child, you know?'

'He was out Tuesday night,' Hay said.

'Was he?'

'In his Mini.'

'No idea, old man. These walls' – a sweeping gesture – 'six feet thick, can't hear a thing. You'll have to ask him.'

'He has friends locally.'

'I'm sure. Of course he has. Grown up with 'em. Vacations, shooting, fishing; gillies, keepers – oh yes, he knows everyone.'

'Girls too?'

Caspar's jaw dropped. No words came.

'He's not gay?' Skene was incredulous. Hay appeared embarrassed, concerned but ready to commiserate. Judging from Caspar's reaction the detective wondered if the man was about to come out with some archaic cry: 'How dare you, sir!' or 'The idea!' but Caspar was to disappoint him.

'Why should you think that?' he asked carefully.

'The reference to girls seemed to surprise you, sir.'

'You're right. It did. I'd never thought in terms of local girls. He has his own circle of friends in Edinburgh, of course, but here? No, there's no one of his – of our – with his background. On Speyside and Deeside, yes, but this is the only large house in Glen Essan.'

'So he wouldn't mix with local girls.' Skene appeared to address a glass ashtray.

'That's what I said.'

'I mean working-class girls.'

Caspar turned to Hay. 'I don't like the implication. I happen to be custodian of an enormous pile of stone which costs a king's ransom to maintain, and which I'm trying to turn into a business venture so that we can make a few thousand in order to repair the roof and mend the drains and improve the heating. I work my guts out keeping the place from falling down round our ears and your man here suggests I'm a *snob*?'

In the drawing room Milly shuffled the photographs into a neat pile. 'Actually,' she said, 'I'm relieved. If it had been a genuine Farquharson and I'd neglected to insure it at its value, we'd have lost thousands. As it is, it's probably worth no more than the five hundred which I shall claim. It won't be unwelcome.' She smiled sweetly, and studied her own Polaroid. 'The point is that no one in this family knows anything about art so, even if anyone had looked at it hard, they'd have been none the wiser. Even my father didn't care for it, hanging it in a back passage.'

A telephone was ringing in the hall. She excused herself and went out. Fleming and Grant heard her excited cry and exchanged glances. They looked round the room with professional interest but no appreciation. It was large, the plastered walls an indeterminate pale shade, a huge carpet in muted colours with threads protruding here and there, fringed sofas in beige with piped cushions, pictures so dark you couldn't identify the subjects, lots of little tables and china ornaments. Neither man would give any of it house room.

Milly returned. 'My son,' she explained casually. 'I mustn't keep you. I'm most grateful . . . I'm sorry you had to go to all this trouble for a mere copy –'

'What's a copy?' Caspar stood in the doorway, Hay and Skene behind him.

'My dear, you'll never credit it: Mr Fleming has had experts looking at my little Polaroid and what we thought was a Farquharson is a fake!'

'I don't believe it.'

'Look, darling' – Milly swooped at the table holding the photographs – 'here's a print of Farquharson's *Afterglow*, and here's my Polaroid. Look at the footprints in the snow.'

Caspar stared at her as she pushed a magnifying glass at him. 'The –' He stopped, his eyes skittering; he just avoided glancing at Hay and Skene. He trained the glass on one photograph, then the other. 'Yes, the tracks are – different.'

'Left and right, dear! They're wrong in the genuine picture; the boot prints come towards you: right, right, right, left, right. The man who made the copy corrected the sequence, see?'

'There's more to it than that,' Fleming said. 'There's this written report, sir. It's a copy, no doubt about it.'

'Right.' Caspar straightened. 'Our painting is a fake. So the thieves got away with something that was valueless. Nice. I like it.'

'It's possible,' Fleming pointed out, 'that at one time you did have a genuine Farquharson after all, the artist often painted similar compositions of the same subject' – he stumbled as they stared at him – 'and it could be that one of your ancestors, ma'am, replaced it like?'

Milly was amused. 'What you're saying is that my

grandfather or my father could have been short of cash, sold the original and had someone make a copy to fill the gap. That's quite possible, nothing illegal about it.' She smiled at Hay.

He nodded. 'The thieves are going to get a surprise when they try to sell it.'

Fleming said quietly, looking at her but speaking for Hay's benefit: 'You said your son phoned, ma'am?'

'Randy!' Caspar clamped his lips so tight on the word that he could have bitten his tongue.

Hay asked pleasantly, 'Where is he, Mrs Gow?'

'He's travelling. On his way to see a friend in St Andrews, actually. Of course, you wanted to speak to him about his car.'

'Did you tell him that?'

'I didn't. Is it important?'

'I can call him myself.' As if they were engaged in no more than social chit-chat he added, 'Was there some kind of problem at his university?'

She pursed her lips. Caspar stared at her. 'A misunderstanding,' she said, without emotion. 'A young woman had an argument with him – over money, I believe.' The flare of her nostrils showed how distasteful she found this. 'The – woman – went to the police with some ridiculous story but I understand she's decided to drop the charges.'

'Charges of what, ma'am?'

'Violence. She says.'

'He's been home for a while –'

'Nothing to that,' Caspar blurted. 'He –'

'It was better, just for the rest of the term.' Milly overrode her husband loudly.

Hay turned to Caspar. 'If you'd be good enough to show DS Fleming where the painting hung, sir . . .'

'He knows.' Caspar was bewildered.

'We need to take another look at that door,' Fleming said firmly, picking up his cue.

Left with Milly Hay said, 'I'm wondering about your son's girlfriends, ma'am.'

'Why?' She had been controlled, now she was stiff with tension.

'If he talked about your valuables, or what he assumed to be valuable – paintings, jewellery – and the girl passed on the information, it might give us a pointer to the thieves.'

'I wouldn't think so. Edinburgh is some distance away, and he'd never tell a – oh, you mean proper girlfriends! Possibly. This place – well, you've seen it – we have no security; everyone's free to wander around: cleaners, men working in the grounds; doors aren't locked, at least in the daytime. In fact I wouldn't be surprised if that was when the picture was taken: in broad daylight, even my ear-rings. If we weren't here the staff might not pay much attention to a van entering the stable yard. A couple of men could have loaded the painting and driven away and no one thought it remarkable.' She shrugged. 'Even if a member of the staff had come on them actually removing the picture, they could have said they were taking it away for cleaning.'

But difficult for strange workmen to justify their presence in her bedroom. Hay didn't press it. 'So,' he said, as if defeated, 'any involvement of your son's girlfriend has no relevance –'

'He doesn't have –'

'– in this context.'

'Not in any context.' She was cool but he'd seen her eyes flicker.

'Now why did Gow react so strongly at the question about Randal's girls?' Skene asked as they drove towards the gates.

'And the missis is keeping something back,' Hay mused.

'She admitted he's in trouble over – a tart, you reckon?

Think he beat her up? We can find that out soon enough.'

'I was asking Gow about the *local* talent. You know something: for my money, he's got a girl here. Who would know?'

'Malcolm would be a good bet.'

Malcolm had no idea but made the obvious comment: if Randal's parents were being cagey, if there was a girl, she might repay investigation. 'The thing is,' Hay said in sudden pique, 'we're investing a lot of time and energy in a case that will likely turn out to be nothing more than failure to report an accident. If his Mini's marked but he swears he never felt a bump, and there are no witnesses, then we haven't got a leg to stand on.'

Chapter Six

Throughout that afternoon the police were unobtrusive but wires were humming between Auchelie and Edinburgh, people were visited, questions asked, and by the time the school bus came trundling up the glen from Cromack the word was out.

'D'you think this line's secure?' Hayley asked, calling Heather on her mobile.

'I should think so.' Heather's response was so casual as to be suspect but her mother, folding eggs into a cheese sauce, showed no obvious interest. 'It's from *Tess of the D'Urbervilles,*' Heather said loudly. 'I'm not sure of the spelling of that; hang on, I'll go and look.' Safe behind her bedroom door she hissed, 'What the hell d'you mean: is this line secure?'

'We're not being bugged?'

'Hayley Lamont!'

'Only the police were at the castle again and everywhere; they're looking for his girlfriend.' Silence. 'Are you still there? Did you hear? I said –'

'I heard you. What did you tell them?'

'I never saw them. They were questioning his mum and dad.'

'What did *they* say?'

'They said he doesn't have a girlfriend. Not here.'

'Who told you this?'

'My mum.'

'Well, I don't know anything.' The defiance was shaky.

'If they find me . . . I wasn't his girlfriend anyway. How could I know anything?'

'He has one.'

'One what?'

'A girl – in Edinburgh. He never told you?' Hayley was excited and smug. 'The city police are looking for him there. He's been sacked from the university.'

'And that just shows how much you know. How could he be sacked? He went back to med. school yesterday.'

'Well, maybe.' Hayley faltered, unable to correlate the two articles of gossip: that Randal had been expelled and that he had indeed returned to Edinburgh. She rallied. 'It's what I heard.'

'What your mum *overheard*.' Heather was furious that Hayley Lamont should affect to know more about Randal than she did herself. 'He got drunk,' she said loftily. 'I know that because he confided in me – naturally – and he was sent down for the rest of the term. That's it!'

Ruth was mashing sprouts and potatoes, bubble-and-squeak being one of Heather's favourites. 'That was Hayley,' she stated as her daughter returned to the kitchen. Heather blinked, undecided how to react. 'You're all right,' Ruth told her comfortably. 'Whatever happened, you're under age. No responsibility can be attached to you.'

'Have you told them?' Heather was tense.

'There's nothing to tell. There's no harm in a neighbour taking you for a spin now and again.'

'What about Tuesday night when we broke it off?'

Ruth drizzled oil into the frying pan and pushed it on a hot plate. She stood with her back to her daughter, intent on the pan. 'Mum?' Heather pressed, tight as strung wire.

Ruth pushed the frying pan off the heat and turned round, her expression enigmatic, but Heather thought she could interpret it. '*I* was driving!' she cried furiously.

'You weren't.'

'I was! We didn't go up the glen like I told you, we went

down; there's a clearing in the Easter Wood where . . . We said goodbye there and he let me drive home.'

'You can't drive.'

'He was teaching me. I hit the guy and I drove on. Randy was asleep. He woke up. I told him I'd hit a deer.'

Ruth walked deliberately to the cupboard, reached for the bottle of Bell's and a glass, poured a small measure and sipped it neat. 'You're still in love with him,' she said.

'I hate him.' Both spoke like automatons. 'I've got no time for him.' A little more feeling: 'Are you still saying I can't be held responsible?'

Ruth drained her glass and stared at her daughter until, disconcerted, Heather moved to the fridge for a Seven-Up.

'Are you going to tell the police?' Ruth asked.

'Should I?'

'No.'

'Just like that.' She was resentful.

'It's my immediate reaction.' Ruth started to speak more naturally although the sentiments were disingenuous. 'The police are looking for a girlfriend because they think she may be able to throw light on what happened Tuesday evening. And I imagine they're hoping she can tell them where he is now. It's that paint, you see; they know Cummings was run down by a green car. Basically they're interested in Randal, not you. No one knows about you,' she added hastily. 'Except – Hayley?'

'She won't talk.'

'How much have you told her?'

'I haven't told her that I – killed Jimmie Cummings.'

Nice to be trusted, Ruth thought wryly, even if it is with such an outrageous scenario. Not so much a lie as a change of roles. She wondered what Randal had done with the Mini Cooper, and was it he who had suggested that Heather say she had been driving? If it was, she was going to wipe the floor with him.

* * *

'It was stolen,' Randal told his mother when she asked what he'd done with the Mini. He had returned to Blair in time for dinner, driving into the yard in an old Escort, meeting his father as he emerged from the coach house.

'The police have been asking,' Caspar growled once they were indoors.

'Asking what? It's history. She dropped the charge. Had to; it was blackmail, she was trying it on to see what she could make out of it.'

Milly said calmly, 'Your father meant the Cromack police, dear. The man who was killed on the back road had green paint on his clothing so they were looking for drivers of green cars.'

Randal gave an astonished laugh. 'They were after *me*?'

She was shocked. 'They weren't *after* –'

'You had a green car.' It emerged as an accusation from Caspar.

'So have hundreds of other people. The fuzz is welcome to the Mini – when they find it.'

Milly smiled. 'They'll lose interest now. The fact that you've came back shows that you have nothing to worry about. Incidentally they were asking if you had a girlfriend locally.'

They were all very still. Randal licked his lips.

'We didn't know of anybody.' Caspar's tone was light. 'Have you?'

'No.'

This thing is getting him down, Milly thought. The boy looks peaky; now where can we send him for a nice holiday?

'Young Gow is back,' Malcolm said, telephoning Hay at eleven o'clock.

'Ah. And the Mini?'

'He's coming in tomorrow, first thing.'

'Is he indeed. I'll be there.'

* * *

In the station on Friday morning they studied him with cool interest, Hay and Skene seeing a young man with cut-glass features, a public school face was how Hay thought of it: pale hair, well-styled, clear eyes, a large nose and wide mouth; it was a face accustomed to authority but mobile, as prone to anger as to charm.

He was alone, which was a bad sign for the police; it indicated he had no need of support. For his part Randal saw a fat man like someone's uncle, and a thin fellow who looked under-nourished. Neither had any distinctive feature apart from the sharp eyes in which he glimpsed a hint of frustration.

He had run through the theft of the Mini Cooper for them: carelessly he'd left it in a lay-by, the keys in the ignition, when he'd gone to relieve himself in a wood. And yes, he had been out on Tuesday evening; he'd intended going over to the next glen but the pass was blocked and he'd got bogged down on top, had to dig himself out. Of course he carried a shovel in winter, didn't everyone? No, he hadn't been on the back road, he'd gone straight from Blair to the pass and home again, there'd been no point in going elsewhere, and he didn't frequent the village bars.

'He's lying,' Skene said when he'd gone, driving away in an old blue Escort which they regarded moodily.

Hay agreed. 'And no way of proving it until we find the Mini, and even then, if it still exists and isn't a wee cube in a breaker's yard, how much d'you bet the original dent isn't disguised by more recent damage?'

'It won't have gone to a breaker. That would be a weak link.'

'That Escort's old but it still cost a bob or two. You think a medical student's got that kind of cash?'

'Plastic money. He's probably got a high limit. Two thousand would cover the cost. There's no way of disproving his story.'

Hay sighed. 'And what does it boil down to? A hit-and-run and not reporting an accident. A good lawyer would get him off even a manslaughter charge. I don't see that we can do anything more here. The St Andrews people can look for the Mini and check on the pal he says he was visiting there – and you can be sure, since he gave us the name and address so helpfully, that young Gow *was* there. Of course the hit-and-run is more suspect taken in conjunction with the incident in Edinburgh; if the one points to a very nasty temper, maybe the hit-and-run was something more than manslaughter, eh? But the woman has withdrawn the charge and as for Jimmie Cummings, he don't seem to have any friends bar MacPherson, and there were no witnesses . . . We haven't unearthed a girlfriend here . . . Even if we knew that Gow was on that back road on Tuesday evening, there's no proof, and he knows it. So you and me, we go back to more pressing problems and leave young Fleming to solve the mystery of the fake Farquharson, him and his bloody footprints. Maybe he'll turn up something, like young Gow running down Jimmie in retaliation for stealing his mum's ear-rings?'

'Or Jimmie turning nasty when the picture turned out to be a fake?'

There was an atmosphere of anticlimax in the village; with no more exciting developments and no obvious CID presence, reporters attracted by the Cummings death were long since gone and no one was interested in Mrs Gow's stolen painting which wasn't real anyway, while the ear-rings were hardly worth a mention. Young Randal's car had been stolen certainly but not here, and it was all that could be expected in such places as St Andrews or Edinburgh although, as Charlie Innes said to Ruth, it was odd, if thieves were to go to the trouble of stealing a car, that they should choose an old Mini Cooper and not something more upmarket. Opportunism, Ruth said: joy-riders.

On Saturday, with the roads clear, Heather chose to cycle to Hayley's, where Isabel would take the pair to Cromack when she did her weekly shop. The girls were to catch the last bus back to Auchelie at ten but Ruth refused to allow her daughter to cycle home in the dark even on this quiet road; she said firmly that she would meet the bus where it turned round at the lodge.

She was there, waiting, at ten fifteen. A little after ten thirty she saw headlights coming up the road. She was tucked neatly against one of the stone gateposts, leaving the bus plenty of room to turn. She started her engine as it came to a halt and a figure moved to the doorway. With the windows steamed up she couldn't be sure but it had to be Hayley, so was Heather staying put, dreaming and thinking that this was the school bus?

Hayley hesitated at sight of a stationary vehicle with side lights burning, then hurried to her garden gate. The bus started its three-point turn. Ruth threw open her door and shouted. Hayley froze, her hand on the latch of the gate.

'Where's Heather?' Ruth approached, trying not to run. 'Where is she?' Trying to keep her voice level.

The door of the lodge opened and Isabel was silhouetted against the light, 'What's happening?'

'Heather?' Ruth threw a wild glare from the girl to the woman.

'Where is she?' Hayley asked.

'I'm asking *you*!'

'You'd better come inside.' Isabel was grudging, not liking this.

They ignored her. 'You went – You did go to the concert?' Ruth asked fiercely.

'I did. Heather cried off.'

'She never went – Then where is she?'

Hayley couldn't take this. She fumbled with the latch of the gate. Isabel advanced. 'Is she missing, Mrs Ogilvie?'

Ruth stared, stricken. 'Where is she, Hayley? *Please?* You've got to tell me.'

Hayley burst into tears and pushed past her mother. Isabel repeated grimly, 'Come inside do, and let's try to sort this out.'

Chapter Seven

'Charlie? Charlie, I'm sorry, were you in bed?'

'No problem, love. What's wrong?'

'She's missing again – yes, I know it's a repeat, but not really, it's been all day and no one's talking. Hayley knows but you can't – I can't force her – How can I? Isabel's being obstructive, maybe she knows, suspects. Could I ask Milly – I don't know . . . If he's just keeping her out – but then Milly's against it too –'

'Ruth, Ruth!' He'd been trying to interrupt and at last he got through to her. 'Be quiet a minute. Breathe deeply. Now, what makes you think she's with Randal?'

'Of course she is! Hayley won't say, she's shut herself in her bedroom and Isabel refuses to have anything to do with it – well, she says you can't force a child . . . She promised to find out and call me.'

'You're at home?'

'Of course. I'm waiting for her to ring; Heather, I mean, she's got her mobile.'

'Have you tried calling her?'

'Yes, it rings but she won't answer.'

'Maybe she can't. Stay there. I'm coming up.' What on earth had made him say that Heather might not be able to answer? He'd meant she could be in a blind spot, not that there was anything *wrong*.

Snowflakes were in the air as he set out, dancing in his beams. The wind was rising – a bad quarter: out of the north-west. *Was* it a repeat performance and he'd find Heather walking up the road? But this night the road was empty even of deer, and for some reason he didn't welcome the opportunity to be of service; this night he was uneasy.

At Camlet the door was open and she was there in the classic pose of the anguished mother, her hands clasped below her throat. He pushed her inside and closed the door. He'd brought a bottle of malt.

'She'll come soon,' she said, and laughed harshly. 'You brought malt last time, remember? You should have overtaken her on the road.' She sat down close to the stove. 'I'm frozen. It's a cold night. The snow's on again. She's not out in it, is she? If they'd broken down she'd have used her mobile. He's got one too.'

He took off his down jacket and put it round her shoulders. He poured whisky for them both and added a smidgen of water. 'First tonight?' he asked convivially, needing to know how much of this was the product of alcohol.

She looked distractedly at the table where there were catalogues and coloured crayons and some kind of plan. No glass. 'I haven't been drinking,' she said, surprised. 'I had to drive. I was planning a garden.'

'Tell me what's happened.'

'I told you over the phone.' She hadn't, and now, questioning, he extracted the details, starting with the original arrangement for the girls' transportation to and from Cromack. 'They must have arranged it yesterday,' she said miserably. 'Hayley told Isabel at breakfast today that Heather wasn't going to the concert after all, that she was going to Aberdeen with me this afternoon. Whether she did tell Hayley that or they invented the story between them I can't find out.' Her voice was rising dangerously. 'Charlie, if Hayley knows where she is, she has to tell me, doesn't she?'

'Morally speaking, yes, but you did say that she can't be forced.' Ruth slumped, letting the jacket fall. Charlie replaced it. 'Look, love, assume that she is with Randal, what's the worst that can happen?' She stared at him blankly. 'You see,' he pressed, 'you've been through it all before: pregnancy, an abortion – whatever your views on abortion, it's not dangerous – and' – he risked grasping this nettle – 'you're not thinking in terms of disease, surely?' He wouldn't say 'AIDS' but he was thinking of the woman in Edinburgh. Word of the prostitute had percolated as if by osmosis.

'Of course not.' It was automatic; she hadn't thought it through. 'I suppose I'm upset because of the deceit,' she confessed. 'That she should have sat here and eaten her breakfast and I said I hoped she'd enjoy the concert, to be sure to call me if she missed the last bus, not to take a taxi, and she promised and went off on her – Charlie! She had arranged to meet him somewhere. Where's her bike?'

'In a hedge or a shed. Behind the supermarket. It's immaterial.'

'What do we do? Just sit and wait?'

He thought of Hayley and was consumed by rage. 'You're staying here by the phone,' he said coldly, concealing his fury. 'I'm going to speak to Isabel.'

There were lights in the lodge. Charlie knocked and the door opened immediately. His car had been heard. Isabel looked frightened. She didn't ask him why he'd come calling at close on midnight. 'Hayley knows where they went,' he said without preamble, no argument about it.

'She won't talk to me.'

'There's a way round that. I can go and ask Mrs Gow. Randal will have told her where he was going, when he expected to be back. If he intended going to Deeside, wherever, and staying out late, he'd have said. It's snowing hard now, that'll be a blizzard on top. If they've run into trouble on the pass, they'll be in urgent need of help. You go up to Hayley now and tell her that her friend may be lying injured somewhere and only she knows which way they went. Either that or I go and get Mrs Gow out of bed and tell her your girl's withholding information that could save her son's life.'

'You don't think –' Isabel was terrified. It had worked. As she left the room Charlie felt blindly for a chair. His own words came back to him and he realized that what had been intended as emotional blackmail could well be the truth. Was this why Ruth was panicking?

Hayley knew nothing, nothing helpful. She confessed to her mother that Heather had said she'd 'made it up' with Randal and that she'd agreed to meet him. She'd told Hayley what she should say to Isabel and she said that she'd be in Cromack by ten and they'd come back on the bus together and no one would be any the wiser. Except that she hadn't been at the bus station and Hayley knew that she was going to have to cover for her friend, but she'd not reckoned on Ruth's distress. Hayley was a very frightened girl – but by first light next morning her state of mind was nothing compared with Ruth's outright terror. Charlie, who had stayed the night at Camlet, was deeply concerned.

At the castle Milly woke feeling that a weight had been lifted from her mind. The woman in Edinburgh had withdrawn the charges, Randal might be allowed back in med. school before the end of term . . . It was snowing again but that would keep him at home, she saw too little of her son nowadays. She went downstairs in her quilted dressing gown to make early morning tea for all of them and someone hammered on the great door. She opened it to Charlie Innes who asked where Randal was. His manner, his drawn features allied to the time – seven thirty – rendered her speechless. Dumbly she gestured to the stairs. She closed the door out of habit and shivered in the cold hall.

'Is there somewhere warm?' Charlie asked, belatedly remembering that Milly was a mother too.

They went to the kitchen, the only truly warm place in

any of these houses. Automatically she lifted the electric kettle, then stopped on her way to the sink and faced him.

'Do you know where he went?' Charlie asked.

She shook her head, then made a grab at the last of her reserves: 'What interest do you have –'

'You were expecting him back last night?'

'He *is* back. He's here, upstairs.' She checked, not wanting to hear more, dreading it but compelled to know: 'Why are you here?'

'Heather is missing. She didn't come home last night.'

She inhaled sharply and Charlie flinched, knowing why men were blindfolded before execution. And even with that terrible gaze she could still say coldly, 'What does that have to do with my son?'

'She was with him.'

'I'm going upstairs. I have to get dressed. I'll look in on Randal. I must take him a cup of – Thank you for calling – Caspar – my husband –' She didn't know what she was saying.

Charlie said gently, 'We have to know where they are. If they've had an accident they need help. Heather hasn't called home, you see, and apparently Randal hasn't either. We must start looking for them, Milly.'

She gasped something and made for the door. Charlie swore in frustration and stood, undecided; he could hardly follow her upstairs. He filled the kettle and switched on. After a few moments Caspar came in, tying his dressing gown, putting on a show of anger which Charlie guessed was masking fear. 'What's this?' he barked. 'Can't make head nor tail of what she's saying. What about Randal?'

'Where is he, Caspar?'

'Why, upstairs of course. In his bed. Where else would he be?'

'Have you looked?'

'What? You calling me a liar?'

'I asked if you'd looked.'

Caspar gasped. 'You're being hostile. Why?'

'He's with Ruth's daughter and neither of them came home last night.' Another shocking possibility occurred to Charlie: that the man was asleep upstairs and that Heather – and then Milly came back, still in her dressing gown, and her face told it all. She addressed Charlie, ignoring her husband.

'Where did they go?'

'Who? What?' Caspar was in denial.

'He's with Heather Ogilvie,' Milly told him, speaking as if he were a child.

'No! Impossible!'

'Her age isn't important, dear, not any longer. They're *missing*; we have to find them.'

'They could be holed up somewhere,' Charlie pointed out, hopefully now. 'It snowed last night, it could have been a blizzard elsewhere. They might be in a hotel.'

'Randal has a mobile.'

'Try ringing him,' Charlie prompted.

'I'll do that!' Caspar was taking charge and blustering, grabbing for the telephone, dialling savagely. 'As for' – he glared at Charlie – 'your suggestion: it's fantastic, monstrous! He'll be staying the night with one of his friends or he's back in Edinburgh. Or St Andrews . . .'

They waited, watching his face. He waited, gripping the receiver. 'No reply,' he grunted. 'Switched off. He's asleep – naturally. He's a late riser.'

At nine o'clock Ruth could bear it no longer and, without consulting the Gows or Charlie, who had left for the pass, she called the police station. Malcolm said he'd try the hospitals but she'd done that already.

The snow had stopped before dawn and the ploughs were out, clearing the roads for the expected influx of skiers. Ruth tried to convince Malcolm that the drivers of the ploughs should be told to look out for a Mini Cooper – a blue Escort, he corrected – but she didn't falter: 'And patrol cars,' she insisted. 'Can't you broadcast an alert on local radio and TV?'

'Mrs Ogilvie! They could be – could have gone to a late-night party and stayed over with friends. She could be home any time.'

There was a tense silence, then: 'She's fifteen. He's twenty-two. He's abducted her; it's a criminal act.'

'It could be,' he agreed tentatively. '*If* she's with him and *if* there's a sexual relationship, and if –'

'There is.'

'You know that?' Initially aroused, he saw that this could be a ploy to force him to take action.

'She talked about marriage. As soon as we found out, Mrs Gow and I insisted they stop seeing each other. But Hayley Lamont says Heather told her they'd made it up again. She told Hayley she was meeting him yesterday.' She went on to give him the details of the plan that had deceived both Isabel and herself. Charlie came in while she was talking and, seeing he had something to tell her, she asked Malcolm to hold the line. He did so, staring out of the window at sunshine weakened by a high cloud layer advancing from the north, wondering which was more likely: that they'd met with an accident or that they were sleeping off the after-effects of a party. Two young people with two mobiles, and no reports of smashes, leastways the type that could incapacitate the pair of them . . . He reckoned they'd partied late. Of course there could be a charge pending regarding sex with a minor but cross that bridge when we come to it; what mattered at this moment was placating Ruth Ogilvie. 'We're going to search for them ourselves,' she said savagely. 'The Gows are out already, and their staff. Charlie Innes wants to speak to you.'

'We're taking this seriously, Tom.' There was a warning in Charlie's voice, indicating that the police should do so too. 'I'm surprised Mrs Gow hasn't been on to you.'

'Maybe she's thinking of the age difference.' Malcolm was dry. He didn't like being told how to do his job and he wasn't about to make allowances for Charlie Innes who was no blood relation to the girl even if he was courting the mother.

'That's a side-issue right now,' Charlie said, not looking at Ruth.

'I'll contact Cromack,' Malcolm said, adding in extenuation: 'You see, the Gows haven't reported him as missing, so it's possible they don't want to – yet. You and Mrs O. could be pulling in the opposite direction to his parents. You follow?'

'Oh, for –' Charlie stopped short, still unwilling to meet Ruth's avid eyes as he listened to Malcolm assuring him that everything would be done once he had the word from his superiors, reminding Charlie that he was only a sergeant; implicit in that was the fact that Charlie was no more than a civilian and should leave this kind of thing to the professionals. Young Gow was getting to Malcolm.

Charlie replaced the receiver and gave Ruth the gist of the exchange. 'We'll make a fresh pot of coffee,' he said, 'and sandwiches, and then we're going out. We'll keep in touch with the police.'

'And the Gows.'

They stared at each other. 'Yes,' she said reluctantly, 'at some point I have to meet Milly. There's nothing we can say to each other of course; none of us knows anything, and she's not responsible for her son, not for his present behaviour. All the same . . .'

'It's awkward,' he conceded, 'but you're right, you have to meet, and sooner rather than later or it looks as if you're avoiding them, and that implies blame.'

She turned to the stove, both knowing that they were indeed apportioning blame yet both tacitly acknowledging that, even if Randal were at fault, his parents were at this moment experiencing the same anguish as Ruth; and Charlie too to a lesser extent.

They searched separately and without any organization.

The Gows were out, no one knew where, Archy MacBean was out in a Blair Land Rover; Isabel wouldn't allow her husband to join the searchers so Hayley stayed at the lodge to look after him, while Isabel held the fort at Blair, where she wouldn't have been normally on a Sunday but someone had to be there for messages: a kind of clearing house. Charlie had chosen to go back to the pass while Ruth went down the back road to the Easter Wood before it occurred to her that if they had met with trouble on a forest track it would be on a newly made road or one where the trees had been felled, and on a slope where there was nothing to stop or hold a car that had plunged over the edge. It wasn't until she started to climb on snow and had to engage four-wheel drive that she knew she wasn't thinking straight. No Escort could have gone high in these conditions – but then, if they'd gone up before the snow came and been trapped, or started down in a blizzard and slid off the road . . . So many places to look, so many convex slopes where a car could be in the bottom of a ravine and hidden from above. Several times she broke into dry sobs, stopped the Land Rover and got out and shouted, as much to relieve the unbearable tension as to hope to reach her daughter. But there was always that chance. By two o'clock she was exhausted and her vision was blurring; if she didn't give up she knew that she could drive over the edge herself. Besides, she had no mobile, she needed to get back to the glen to find a telephone.

Charlie (who did have a mobile) was in Strathdon and he had no news. She asked him to try to contact the Gows, which he could do by way of Isabel. Meanwhile she rang the police at Auchelie only to be told by a strange female voice that Malcolm was in Cromack but, so far as her informant knew, there was no police search in progress. Nor did the woman know if Randal Gow had been reported missing.

Ruth waited in the phone box, certain that she was being stonewalled, seeing that it was starting to rain, praying: Please God, tell me where she is; don't let her be out in this, God, not injured – and she was a person who thought herself a humanist.

Charlie came back to her. From Isabel he'd learned that the Gows were still driving the roads on this side of the county and would stay out until Randal was found. Ruth didn't bridle at the omission of Heather's name, each to her own. Milly – it was she who had called Isabel asking for messages – had said she'd reported Randal as missing; she'd spoken to the police in Cromack.

'Are the police going to do anything?' Ruth asked.

'They have nothing to go on.' Charlie's voice was interspersed with static. 'They are looking for the Escort however.'

'We should push it, Charlie: insist he's abducted her, bring a charge. Maybe then they'll pull their fingers out. Like rape and murder – anything; just *find* them!'

'Well, love, the two of them were friendly. The police know that now. Everyone knows.' She sighed in despair. 'Ruth, go home. I'll meet you there. This is needle-in-haystack stuff. Let's hope they're shacked up in Aberdeen or somewhere.' A long silence. 'You still there, love?'

'I'm here.'

'We'll meet back at Camlet. You're not doing any good out in this' – there was sleet in the rain now and she thought it could be snowing where he was – 'you're just exhausting yourself, wasting energy –'

'What else can I do?'

'We go home, have a hot meal, rest a while.' Pleading was no good so he'd take charge. 'I need food, we both do. Will you start home now?'

'It'll be light for hours yet.'

'After we've eaten we'll go to Blair and make a plan with the Gows. They have to give up sometime and come in. Milly has pull with the police. We'll work out how – a helicopter! Had you thought of that?'

He was right. Searchers in a chopper could look into all those otherwise hidden places in the gorges: under overhangs, in deep water – no, not water.

'I'll come back,' she assured him, firmer now, even excited. 'I'll see you there and we will go up to the Gows. Tell Isabel, Charlie, tell her to contact Milly; we have to organize a proper search.'

There was no more animosity between Milly and Ruth than there would be between mothers on opposing sides in a war. Seduction and blame were nothing compared with the compulsion to find their children, to save them if they were at risk.

'Caspar won't come home,' Milly told them as they drank tea in the kitchen. 'Leave him' – as if anyone had proposed finding him – 'he'll probably sleep in the Range Rover.'

'The police are dragging their feet,' Charlie said, pouring the remains of his whisky into his tea.

Ruth regarded their host incuriously, noting that people did indeed age in hours even if hair didn't turn white; surely those were new lines between Milly's nose and mouth, lines that would never be smoothed out again. Her hair wasn't combed, but then had Ruth combed her hair today?

'They're not dragging their feet,' Milly said. 'They find the situation delicate.'

'Naturally,' Ruth put in. 'They're concerned with politics.'

'Caspar told the chief constable that he didn't give a damn about any alleged relationship with a minor, what he demanded was that they find his son.'

'I was thinking a helicopter might be useful,' Charlie said.

Milly's eyes sharpened. 'So you don't go along with the police and subscribe to the theory that they've . . .'

'Eloped?' Ruth supplied. 'Done a runner? I wish they had.'

'So do I.' They were on the same wavelength. Milly added dolefully, 'But if that were the case Randy would have phoned me, even with a string of fibs, if only to let me know he was safe.'

'But would he phone if he was with Heather?' Charlie asked curiously.

She wasn't disconcerted. 'He's family orientated, but to his own family. He'd still phone to reassure me even if he didn't give a thought to Ruth.'

'So what you're saying is that even if Heather's with him, he'd phone you.'

'What you're both saying,' Ruth broke in stridently, 'is that since he hasn't phoned, they're not safe in some tacky hotel or a squat or on someone's floor.'

'He'd have called me,' Milly insisted. 'We'll have a helicopter tomorrow. I've been in touch with a firm.'

Ruth closed her eyes in contrition. 'I'm sorry, I shouldn't have said that.'

'We're both in the same boat,' Milly reminded her. 'The other thing doesn't matter; as Caspar said: they can do anything; Randal can stand trial, go to prison . . . They can get married. I'd be happy . . .'

She didn't finish. It was unnecessary, they heard the words in their minds: 'just as long as he's alive.' And Heather too, of course.

Dusk came early that Sunday afternoon. Clouds dropped and consolidated and by four o'clock it was snowing heavily. Caspar called Blair to say he was at the Spittal of Glenshee, coming home by way of the Devil's Elbow; there was nothing he could do, visibility was down to a few yards and deteriorating. Milly told him to stay where he was, put up at one of the hotels; a helicopter would be out tomorrow, searching. He asked if that meant there was some indication that Randal wasn't on a road and pointed out that the Escort was only a car, not a four-track; he must be on a surfaced road. Evidently Caspar had blocked out the possibility that the car had left the road by accident or, like everyone else, he was just plain exhausted and past rational thought.

Charlie would have preferred to go back to Camlet, not that anywhere could be comfortable this terrible afternoon, with the light fading rapidly and a swirling white world beyond the castle walls, but Isabel had gone home and Ruth wouldn't leave Milly alone in that great empty place.

In fact Milly had found an address book in Randal's room, little-used but with some telephone numbers, and she was trying to trace his friends on the off-chance that he had called one of them, or that someone might put forward a suggestion as to where he might be. Those people at home on a Sunday responded with more numbers and now both women were busy on the telephones, Ruth using Charlie's mobile.

With the land-line in use Sergeant Malcolm was unable to get through and it was with a ghastly sense of foreboding that Charlie, drifting through the hall, looked out of a window to see a ghostly police car come to a stop on the forecourt. He opened the door to Malcolm who glanced furtively into the hall. 'They've found the car,' he whispered.

Chapter Eight

The Escort was in a large car park which served several ski lifts, the main one going to the summit of a peak called Maddy Rigg. A small complex at the foot consisted of a café, a shop that also hired out skiing equipment, and the usual offices and lavatories, all necessitating the employment of security guards at night. One of these, a former policeman, had seen the Escort when he came on duty at five o'clock yesterday afternoon but he'd thought nothing of it because, although it was dusk and snowing and the lifts weren't running, other cars were there belonging to staff and a few late customers in the café.

This morning the snow was deep, the ploughs hadn't come through and the guard, alone except for his German Shepherd, turned in on one of the camp beds provided for emergencies. At eleven the first plough arrived followed by conscientious members of staff in a Range Rover who provided the guard and his dog with breakfast. A widower, he had no commitments at home so he put in a few hours' overtime digging out a route to the bottom of the main lift. It wasn't until late afternoon, when a plough was trying to clear the car park and the driver came in to ask whose car was buried out there, that the guard realized no one had claimed the Escort. With his police connections he discovered the registered owner quite quickly; it took rather longer to ascertain that the car hadn't been stolen – the first thought – but had been taken in part exchange by a garage in St Andrews, and sold on only three days ago to a Randal Gow of Auchelie.

The three people at Blair listened to Malcolm's account without comment and with varying emotions: bewilderment, disbelief, mounting horror, denial.

'She's not with him,' Ruth breathed. 'She doesn't ski.'

Milly left the room in a rush. Malcolm's eyes followed her. 'Does *he*?' he asked quietly.

'I think so.' Ruth was vague. 'He goes to Switzerland.'

Charlie studied her face. Had they made a colossal mistake? If Heather was not with Randal was that good or bad? He preferred her to be with him: better the devil you know . . .

Milly returned. 'His skis are still here.' She looked ill. 'Why would he go to Maddy Rigg and not ski?'

Malcolm had a thought but was reluctant to voice it and then have to follow through. Charlie had no such qualms.

'Did they go in the café?'

'I don't know.' Malcolm was wary. 'I don't know whether they were together.' He was obviously uncomfortable.

'You call them, Charlie,' Ruth ordered, not trusting herself to speak to strangers, not sure of the questions.

He found the number and dialled, staring at the white world beyond the window panes, knowing that the ski centre would have closed down long ago with no lifts running. The guard answered – MacAllister, the same man who had reported the Escort. Even as he started to speak Charlie knew the fellow was more concerned in justifying his own action in not reporting the car sooner than in tracing the driver. He didn't learn much when he'd overcome that barrier, and how could he? Yesterday morning, before the snow came, the ski lifts had been running, the café full of people, how would anyone know which of them belonged to the Escort?

Charlie said he understood that but did anyone ever take the lift, the main lift say, when they didn't intend to ski, just for the view from the top, and then walk down? MacAllister said they didn't, that is, people did go up for the ride, the management were talking about a café at the top too, in order to attract custom during the summer, but these sort of people didn't walk down, they'd stay a while and catch the next lift to the bottom.

'When did the lift stop running yesterday?'

'When the cloud came down,' said MacAllister. 'That would be around three, three thirty.'

Malcolm took over then and asked for the name and number of the chap who had been at the top station of the main lift on Saturday. Telephoned at his home the fellow remembered a couple who had ridden to the top without skis around noon: tourists, he said, except that the man was carrying a pack, but both wearing the kind of clothing that told him they'd be going down again at the first opportunity. He'd remembered them because the girl was very pretty with 'like diamonds in her hair' and they'd been hugging each other when they came off the lift. He guessed they were honeymooners or something. He'd looked out for their return but he'd not seen them – which was odd because everyone else skied down from the top and the lift usually returned to the bottom empty. He should have seen them.

It was the 'diamonds' that clinched it; Heather's favourite Alice band was set with marcasites. The conclusion seemed obvious; they'd wandered away from the top station, the cloud came down and they couldn't find the way back. They'd been out there for two days and a night in blizzard conditions.

This was no longer work for the police but for Mountain Rescue, and they called the shots. It was nearly dark now and snowing hard, it would be a gale above three thousand feet. There could be no search that night.

The local team managed to get through behind a plough to assemble at the ski centre where they bedded down on floors. During the night another civilian team and the RAF arrived and by dawn there were upwards of a hundred qualified searchers ready to start. They divided: one team going up that facet of the mountain above the road, the others to rolling wastes of snow out to the side where there was a long ski run that Randal might be familiar with. Here there were depressions where drifts were deep enough to conceal all signs of a body. Because that was what they thought they were searching for: two days and two nights now, and it had transpired that neither youngster was a mountaineer. Gow was no more than a downhill skier and the girl not even that; they had no equipment and no proper clothing. Unless they had found shelter they couldn't have survived. There was no shelter on Maddy Rigg other than the top station and they weren't there, at least, there was no answer from the outside telephone.

The search was by no means perfunctory but in the continuing high winds it couldn't be thorough. Snow had covered tracks that had been made on Saturday, and any discarded clothing. That last would be significant because in the final stages of hypothermia people sometimes strip, but the rescue dogs turned up nothing. Apart from visiting the terminal the first team didn't stay on top; after the exhausting plod to the station through waist-deep drifts, after two men had been blown over, they stayed below the summit ridge. There was no question of bringing in a helicopter.

Back at Auchelie they waited, Isabel and two of her cleaners at the castle, Charlie at Camlet after a brief foray to feed his hens. With Ruth he visited Milly, to find her spruced up and the kitchen tidy, venison marinating on the side. Isabel was pulling her weight, trying to establish a semblance of normality. Caspar hadn't come home but he kept in touch, traversing the Grampian roads, presumably in some kind of forlorn hope that Randal had come down to the wrong glen. No one questioned his reason for staying out, rather they were glad of his absence. The principals were learning how to cope; a fragile skin of convention had formed, masking horror. Caspar was an unknown quantity, he could break the skin.

Seeing Archy enter the stable Charlie went out to find him attending to the horse. Archy, who had been out on the roads yesterday, said he was keeping busy; Lamont expected to be back tomorrow, meanwhile he was glad to do everyone's job, he needed to: 'What I really want is to be out there looking for her, but they'll only take climbers.'

'It's to do with insurance,' Charlie lied, thinking that Archy's expertise on the hill would surely be useful but the edict had gone out: no volunteers unless qualified rescuers.

'I've got two lambs,' Archy said. 'She made me promise to let her see the first.'

'So you said.' Charlie turned away, he couldn't bear it; the man's eyes were watering. 'They'll find her,' he muttered.

'All alone up there!' Archy exclaimed. 'At night! Snowing. She'd have been so feared.'

'They were together,' Charlie said, but doubtful about it. Even if they'd been together to start with, they could have lost touch in the cloud.

Archy was silent. The man's mind wasn't here, in the stable at Blair, he was up there, with a child – virtually – alone in the blizzard. 'Archy.' No response. 'Archy!'

'Yes?'

'Ruth is suffering too. And I loved – love Heather as well. We're all together in this. You're not alone, man.'

Archy's face was like stone. 'She was,' he said.

At five o'clock the search was called off. When the last team straggled in word came to Auchelie that they would be ready to go out at first light next morning and that their numbers would be augmented by two more teams: an extra eighty searchers. At Camlet there was little reaction to the news; the mood was one of quiet depression shot though with flashes of feverish excitement when Ruth, studying the map, would see that there was a ruin marked in a glen at the back of Maddy Rigg, or she'd wonder if Heather wasn't with Randal at all but had left him, come down and run away, as children do for no reason, or even that the Escort was a ploy: they'd dumped it and fled abroad to start a new life together, which they couldn't do here because Heather was a minor. And then she'd remember that they'd been seen on top of Maddy Rigg, the hectic moment would die and depression ooze back, now intensified.

On the Tuesday the skies cleared, the sun came out, the lifts were operating again and the skiers warned to look out for any sign of the missing pair. But they were on sections already searched; now the area had widened to the vast massif beyond the top station where no one went because it led nowhere, only to an untracked wilderness, pristine and alien. Or so it appeared to Charlie, stepping out of the lift on the summit, having the features pointed out to him by a rescuer before the man followed his team down the ridge, heading for those cheerless snowfields.

At Blair they had discussed going to Maddy Rigg. Ruth and Milly didn't voice their reluctance but it was obvious from their lack of expression that they would find the experience harrowing. 'Would we do any good,' Ruth asked, 'just going up and coming down again?'

Charlie visualized her on top of the mountain looking at what would be the view in normal times but which now would present itself as a dreadful hell in which her child could be suffering appallingly, or had suffered. The same for Milly, of course.

'I'll go,' Caspar said heavily, but in the end it was Charlie who'd gone, Milly having insisted that Caspar should go back to bed. He had come home last night looking as if he'd neither slept nor washed for a week, oddly subdued – Charlie had never known Caspar quiet until now – deferring to Milly, apparently unable to formulate any course of action although at some point he had been at the ski complex and had given permission for the Escort to be forcibly entered. The boot contained an old oil-stained anorak, a jack, wheelbrace and two mobiles. Since there were no keys the car could be removed only by hot-wiring it, or with a recovery vehicle. Caspar said it should be left where it was until he'd spoken to Randal's mother. At Blair they had listened to this in bewilderment, unable to focus on something so trivial as the disposal of an old car. They were more concerned with the helicopter which would be flying today but the prevailing mood was of hopelessness; at some point they would have to accept that nothing would be found until all the snow had melted.

They hadn't made allowances for the strength of the sun at this time of year. It needed only a few hours of warmth for the new powder to melt leaving the ridges and high rocks exposed and there, caught between two stones, a glove was found by one of the dogs.

It was red, woollen and sodden. It could have been dropped by anyone or blown from the ski lift, but the helicopter was called in from where it had been working down the line of a burn to the north, the winchman picked up the glove and within a short time it was at Blair.

Yes, Ruth said dully, stroking the glove as if it were animate, it belonged to her daughter, and the winchman gave Charlie a map reference before the helicopter took off, making for the area which was now the focal point.

At Blair they spread a map on the kitchen table and, using the grid reference, saw that the glove had been found at about two thousand feet on a spur running in a north-westerly direction from the summit of Maddy Rigg.

Archy MacBean was splitting logs in the yard, and Milly called him indoors and showed him the map. Caspar was staring blindly at it as if he'd never been taught to map-read. Archy too was stymied, he found his way among the hills like an animal, by instinct and memory; maps and compasses were less of a closed book to him than unnecessary, at least on his home ground.

It was Charlie who made the effort to interpret the new development. 'They were descending,' he ventured: 'getting down to lower ground –' He stopped, uncertain where this was leading, but none of the others was hanging on his words. He thought they had given up hope. He looked at Caspar. 'It's a north-west ridge,' he said meaningly.

Randal's father raised lacklustre eyes. 'So?'

Archy said, 'The wind was in the north-west that afternoon. They'd never walk into it! They'd turn their backs to it. Anyone would.'

Ruth bent over the map. 'The lift's on the south face. They were walking away from it.'

Caspar came to life. 'The cloud was down; that's why the lift stopped running. They were lost in the fog. You turn round once and you lose all sense of direction.'

He was right. Although none of them was a mountaineer – even Archy would think of himself as merely a hillman – they were all accustomed to mountain mists, and Caspar went out after the deer; they knew how easy it was to lose one's way in the cloud.

There was a sudden clatter as Archy broke away from their circle, knocking over a chair, plunging for the back door. Charlie glimpsed him rounding a corner of the coach house and then he was gone. No one commented on his behaviour.

'Where does this ridge lead?' Ruth asked.

Charlie turned to the map resignedly and then he stiffened. 'He could be making' – he faltered, aware of the inappropriate tense – 'for this bothy – or ruin? There's something marked –'

'It's a house!' Milly cried.

'I don't think so. There's not even a path marked to it, let alone a track. Anyway, someone will have spotted it by now. It will have been eliminated' – bad word – 'the chopper could have been there already.'

'All the same,' Ruth put in, 'if he had a map, he could have been making for it. That could be why they chose to go down that ridge.'

Charlie looked at Caspar and thought that they could be thinking the same thing: that even if the couple had come out below the cloud, even if they had a map, they wouldn't have seen the ruin – whatever it was – because it was snowing. And why should Randal have a map? They'd only taken the lift for the ride; Heather was even wearing trainers. And why should they make for an anonymous speck on the map that must be some four miles away from where the glove was found when the ski complex was only a mile below the top station? But they couldn't find the top station . . . Nevertheless there had to be some explanation as to why they walked into the gale.

The team that had found the glove continued down the north-west ridge, which was now curving westward, people below the crest with dogs in case their quarry had drifted sideways in the cloud. They looked for other articles of clothing and the feeling was that they should move quickly since, by some unforeseen set of circumstances, the pair might still be alive. There was a chance that one of them might have remembered something: something heard, something read, about building a snow cave. They could be lying up like hibernating animals, and just alive. Strange things happened in mountains and until bodies were found you didn't abandon the last vestiges of hope.

The ridge ran out into high moorland: great clumps of heather, and boulders capped by wet snow. There were signs of a path and they knew that in the glen ahead a disused track ran to the ruins of a shieling which to the naked eye was indistinguishable from the rocks about it. The helicopter crew had reported no sign of life there.

The chopper had left to refuel and the searchers assembled on the moor to determine how best to cover the huge area to south and west. As they talked a collie broke away and the other dogs and the men watched him go straight to a snowy boulder where he sniffed excitedly, stood back and started to bark.

They plunged towards him, dreading the first sight but trained to accept it, knowing relief because at last it was over – and then remembering that if two bodies were not here then it wasn't over.

They hadn't found the first body. What the collie had discovered was a rucksack: a dark blue shade, which was why the helicopter had missed it. It was a large pack, the main compartment open and empty, but in a side pocket there was an inexpensive camera: a Canon, still in its case. The film would be developed but it would tell them nothing; they needed help now: to know what had happened after the pack and camera were abandoned. They assumed the rucksack had contained clothing, which implied that someone had had the sense to put it on, but was either of them thinking clearly at this point? The camera wasn't worth much – say fifty or sixty pounds – but it weighed nothing, it could have been slipped in a pocket. It was pointed out that they were only assuming it was Gow's rucksack, so contact was made with Blair, and now it was Milly who was forced to identify objects and confirm that they belonged to her son.

'We knew when they found the glove,' Caspar said. 'I mean, we knew they were descending that ridge.'

'Where is he?' Milly asked. He stared at her in consternation. 'It was rhetorical, dear,' she assured him, feeling a rush of pity, feeling that she was selfish, as if she were appropriating all the grief to herself. 'And then there's Ruth,' she said, staying on the same tack. 'Poor Ruth.' She had returned to Camlet with Charlie. Milly rang them with the latest information.

'They got off the mountain,' Ruth told Charlie, replacing the receiver. 'The rucksack was found on moorland. Let's go round there tomorrow and get as close as possible. There must have been a path to that shieling at one time. At least we'll be on the move. Well, why don't you say something? You're against my going. Why, Charlie?' He wouldn't meet her eye. She went on coldly, 'You don't want to come; all right, I'll go on my own, but you might as well tell me why; I can't feel worse than I do already.'

'That's the point,' he admitted. 'You want to go because you think you can find her when the teams, and dogs, and the chopper can't. That's unreasonable and when you see that country you'll know I'm right, and you'll feel worse than you do now.'

'I *want* to hurt.'

'I know you do but you have to – everyone feels the same: all parents in this kind of situation.'

'You're saying she's dead.'

He hesitated. 'One of the rescuers told me that it's painless. They feel warm – which is why they discard clothing – and they feel tired, so they lie down and go to sleep.'

She listened and understood, and agreed. 'But he was talking about the final stages,' she pointed out. 'He didn't tell you what it was like when she was still conscious of what was happening: the time between knowing they were lost and when she – as you so kindly put it – lay down in the snow and went to sleep. If I stay here I shall go mad.'

He had never suggested a sedative, had known she would refuse it. Now he thought that exhaustion might act as a drug and he agreed to go for that reason, and because there was no question of her going alone. He called Blair and told Caspar what they intended doing. Caspar said he couldn't leave Milly and asked where Charlie proposed to start. He said Ruth wanted to reach the ruined shieling, and Caspar agreed, but without conviction, that if there had been a lull in the blizzard, Randal could have seen the ruin and mistaken it for a bothy, a place that would provide shelter.

'Was he carrying a map?' Charlie asked.

'I wouldn't think so. Why should he? They were only

riding up on the lift and coming down again. Why would he take a map?'

'Quite.' About to end it there, Charlie checked. 'So why was he carrying a rucksack?'

'There was the camera – and clothing. He'd have had his down jacket: bulky thing; he'd have taken that for Heather no doubt. It would be cold on top' – his voice faded – 'I was talking to Charlie, dear.' Silence, he'd covered the mouthpiece. Charlie waited patiently. Caspar came back. 'Milly says keep in touch.'

'I take it Milly's not going out,' Charlie told Ruth who was making sandwiches, concentrating on food, on anything rather than the horror that threatened to engulf her. She made no comment on Milly's intentions, or lack of them.

'You can't go now,' Charlie protested, eyeing the preparations. 'It's too late.' And knew that any time was too late.

'These can go in the fridge. We'll leave before dawn and start walking at first light.'

The organizers of the search had had the same idea and on the Wednesday morning teams converged to search the area where the rucksack had been found, taking in the shieling and the glen to its west. At the mouth of the glen there was a surfaced road but since it served no houses it wasn't maintained and after a mile or two it ended at a turning circle. Charlie and Ruth arrived at six o'clock to find two RAF Land Rovers there already, men standing about, and a civilian team coming in as Charlie parked. He was concerned for Ruth, guessing that whatever happened it wouldn't be good.

She weathered the initial hostility well, an RAF sergeant approaching to ask their business, thinking they were Press, disconcerted when Charlie introduced Ruth. There was no way she could be stopped from trying to reach the shieling, and had there been, no one here would have attempted it. The sergeant pointed out that there was no proper track, addressing Charlie, pleading. Charlie shrugged, he couldn't stop her either.

They started out, Ruth in wellingtons, Charlie in proper walking boots, both drawing aside as more rescuers came up behind them, going faster. After a while the path became ill defined: undrained and slushy, colonized by sedges and cotton grass. Ruth floundered on gamely, remarking once that the going would have been easier with a frost. She stopped then and regarded the rising ground ahead: dark sweeps of heather, and the snows of Maddy Rigg showing over the rim of the moors. She didn't speak again until they reached the shieling which was nothing more than a gable-end and a tumble of stones. She poked about among the stones, thinking that it was not impossible that she might find something of Heather's that men – being men – had missed, but there was only sheep's dung and old chewed snack wrappers. She asked Charlie to find some sheep's wool and when he pulled off her wellingtons her feet were bleeding from broken blisters. He begged plasters from the next rescuers to arrive and when they were plainly annoyed, thinking that they might have to carry out a third victim, he snarled at them and said that this woman would crawl back to the road-end before she asked for help.

Actually with her boots padded she walked back to the Range Rover, if painfully. She admitted that to try to go further than the shieling was to invite disaster, and it was at last borne in on her that hundreds of people were trying to find her daughter, and now, going to the other extreme, she maintained, at least to herself, that she was an encumbrance. They drove back to Camlet, virtually in silence.

The teams stayed out while the light lasted. At six o'clock they packed it in for the day and agreed, as if it were routine, to start again at dawn. On the Thursday two teams tried a new approach: going in from the north. The signs – the glove and the rucksack – had pointed to the couple having veered to the west and even south but there was mention of a slope that was prone to avalanche in the other glen, and there had been those heavy snowfalls at the weekend . . .

The northern glen was uninhabited; a road led to a shooting lodge, unoccupied and shuttered, and a track continued to a bothy, unlocked but untenanted, then came a stalker's path that climbed to a pass. The searchers reached the watershed but they saw no sign of avalanches and they didn't go beyond the pass because the ground dropped away on the other side, and the thinking was that no exhausted walker, having descended from Maddy Rigg, was going to go *up* again. In any event there was no point in rescuers crossing the pass because the moors lay on the other side and that was where the rucksack had been found. Through binoculars they could see sweep searches in progress in the distance. They turned back.

The ravens were spotted about three o'clock: several flying in and appearing to land about two miles from the ruined shieling, an area where no one had searched as yet because it was far away from a line between rucksack and ruin, a line where the search had been concentrated.

She was a few yards from a burn, under an overhanging boulder – which was how the helicopter had come to miss her, if it had flown so far. She lay on her side as if she were asleep and some thought she was at first but she'd been there too long, and the ravens almost as long. Her trainers were incongruous because she was wearing a big padded jacket, the hood up and tied, the elasticized cuffs pulled down over her small bare hands.

They sent for the helicopter, and in the last hour of daylight they started to look for the second body.

Chapter Nine

After one body was found, life for some of those involved became unworldly, or other-worldly. Charlie had been fond of Heather, he adored her mother, so he was concerned but he could be objective, watching Ruth carefully, alert for any sign of collapse. At the same time he was conscious that up at Blair Randal's parents must be still in the deepest throes of suffering. Ruth had some kind of termination but as the days drew out, and the searchers started at dawn, finished at dusk in their grim routine, still there was no sign of Randal.

Heather's shoulder bag was found about a mile from where she died: linen with leather trim, Laura Ashley by way of Oxfam. It contained a comb, tissues, a purse with two five-pound notes and coins, a small key and a plastic holder with photographs cut to fit: two of Randal beside his Mini and one of Ruth in the garden at Camlet, picking Brussels sprouts. Ruth handled the contents reverently, replaced them and took the bag to Heather's room which remained just as she'd left it. Charlie had moved into Camlet but he slept on the sofa in the parlour until such time as Ruth might ask him to share her bedroom. He went back to Cougar daily to see to the hens, hoping that eventually she would accompany him and then he might put out feelers concerning her leaving Camlet for good with all its poignant associations.

At the autopsy water was found in Heather's lungs. It was a measure of Ruth's state of mind that the manner of her daughter's death meant little to her. Even the discovery that she had been six weeks pregnant failed to move her; death had annihilated feeling. News of the pregnancy enraged Charlie at first and then it occurred to him that perhaps the pair had planned to elope after all – as Ruth had suggested at one time – and had been overtaken by the storm, but this was no more than speculation; they were gone, he hoped they'd been happy during their brief affair, but it crossed his mind that it would have been kinder if Randal had stayed with her. But no doubt he didn't know that she was dead, and he had been going for help.

The theory was that they were together until Heather fell in the burn. Both would have been exhausted by that time, battling with the blizzard, but Randal had managed to pull her out of the water. It was possible that she hadn't died immediately, he'd placed her on her side under the overhang but he hadn't expelled the water. At some point, and this was probably back where the rucksack had been opened and abandoned, he had made her put on his down jacket, and now he fitted it round her snugly and left to get help. But of course he never made it and was still out there somewhere: under a peat bank, below a waterfall, invisible both to people on the ground and in the helicopter.

After a further week the search was abandoned. The Escort had been brought down to Blair and Archy MacBean had found Heather's bike in an alder copse on the road a mile from Camlet. It hadn't been obvious but Archy had combed that four-mile stretch between Camlet and the gates of Blair thinking, as Ruth had thought at the shieling, that because he loved the cyclist, her machine would speak to him. Archy had settled into a kind of morose tension, avoiding Ruth and Milly, taking his orders from Caspar. He tolerated Charlie who took him eggs and always inquired after the cats. Whether Archy learned that Heather had been pregnant no one knew and Charlie wouldn't have dared to ask him. In his spare time the man went back to the moors where her body had been found. When Charlie asked him what he did there he said he was looking for ravens which surprised Charlie because he hadn't known that Archy had any feeling for Randal.

The film from Randal's camera was developed and all the exposed shots had been taken around the top station on Maddy Rigg: shots of Heather brimming with fun, of Randal, his eyes eloquent, of them both – evidently on a self-timer since no one came forward to say he'd taken it, of the view with – unmistakably – a bland grey sky to the north, peaks below it already in shadow.

The funeral came and went: the first funeral; Ruth in fine violet tweed, Milly in black, their eyes commiserating with each other, the one for the child now in the earth, the other for the one still to be found. No one mentioned the baby to Milly, not even Ruth who visited at Blair, now feeling compassion for Caspar, for whom she'd had no time before. He was seldom there, going out with his dogs to the moors, still searching, even after the professionals left. Charlie assumed that he looked for ravens as Archy did, and wondered if the two of them met out there and what was said.

In Caspar's absence it was the staff who set about restoring some kind of routine to Blair. After his bout of flu Ian Lamont came back to work: a squat dour Highlander, senior to Archy but wary of him in his present mood. There was a lot to do on the estate with the lambing and the pheasants, with fencing and drainage and general maintenance. As for the grounds, Caspar had been about to take on more gardeners, and the workmen were waiting to resume work on the cascade. Without Caspar, who was to supervise the building of it? Was there to *be* a cascade?

As the permanent men beavered away to keep the estate running, the female staff worked doggedly indoors. Isabel pushed Milly a little more each day, standing guard on occasions such as when Fleming returned, first offering his formal condolences and then reporting progress. Milly threw Isabel a helpless glance.

'He means your picture,' Isabel reminded her. 'The one that was stolen: what hung in the back passage.'

'Ah.' Milly sighed; it was an event from another time, another world. 'The Farquharson.'

'The fake,' Isabel corrected.

'We've been unable to trace it, ma'am,' Fleming told her. 'It'll have been offered to a fence – an illegal dealer – and he'd have turned it down, told the thieves it wasn't genuine.'

'I don't want it back,' Milly said, and shuddered.

He looked at her curiously, not perceptive enough to make the connection: the picture had been mostly snow and Milly would never again view snow with equanimity. When he left she went outside to look at the daffodils which were starting to show colour on the lawns. It was there that Lamont found her and, instructed by Isabel, asked what should be done about the cascade. He took her to see what had been done to date, pointing out that the ground was drying, excavating could be resumed; soon they should be pouring cement – and then there was the landscaping; Mr Gow had talked about taking on seasonal gardeners, decisions had to be made.

'It's too much,' Milly said. Lamont had gone too fast.

'I know what himself wants,' he said. 'I can take over till he feels fit like.' He added slyly, 'Someone has to do it.'

She stared at him. He sounded like her father when ponies had to be groomed, a dog's mess cleared up, pets buried: 'Someone has to do it.' Generations of clansmen were ranged behind her. 'You take over here,' she told him. 'I'll find Mr Gow's plans. He'll be back himself shortly.'

'What I was thinking,' Lamont said.

In Cromack Hay discussed the matter of Jimmie Cummings' death with his superintendent and relayed the result to Skene. The case couldn't be officially closed because it wasn't known exactly how the man had died, that is, although he had been knocked down by a motor car it wasn't known whether it was accidental or deliberate, nor which green car had been involved. None of these questions could be answered now; even if the Mini Cooper were found, and it was dented and the paint matched, Randal couldn't be brought to book. So unofficially the case was closed – thank God; it had been an awkward one.

Spring arrived in Glen Essan. The birch woods were full of primroses, gardens with daffodils. Hedges were greening; the soil dried out, there were lambs everywhere, and Caspar returned, throwing himself into work as if this were his way of driving out demons. The loch, whose outlet was to provide water for the cascade, was deepened, the steps in the slope graded ready for the cement, two extra gardeners were engaged and Milly was persuaded to study catalogues and choose plants for the landscaping. She asked Ruth for help but although both women tried to concentrate on the project they knew that this was displacement activity; neither cared about Caspar's water feature.

One afternoon, coming back through the walled kitchen garden after discussing the pool that was being scooped out at the foot of the cascade, Milly asked Ruth if she could ride. Thinking that someone was needed to exercise Caspar's horse Ruth said she hadn't been on a horse since she was sixteen, and couldn't Milly take the horse out? 'I will,' she said, 'but I'd prefer company. You could hire a pony in the village.'

Ruth agreed tentatively, thinking that it would be something constructive to do, that riding was healthy and it was a good sign that Milly actually wanted to do something.

'We can hire a trailer,' she was saying, staring at a robin shouting cheerfully on the stone wall. 'I'm sure we can manage to hook it up: the two of us.'

Ruth had a premonition. 'Where did you think of going?'

'You can get vehicles as far as the bothy, unload there and ride over the pass. On horseback it's the quickest approach to where – he was lost.'

'Milly!' About to protest, Ruth remembered that for the other woman there was a compulsion to find her son. She went on more quietly, 'All that ground's been covered: by the rescue teams, by the helicopter, by Caspar. Archy MacBean still goes out there.' Privately she was trying to balance the benefit of exercise against the ill-effects of its purpose. 'We could ride in the glen –' she began, and stopped, seeing Milly's eyes fixed, her face reddening –

'MacPherson! This is my *garden*!' She was on her feet, enraged; by a doorway in the wall MacPherson had turned, grinning, his flies open, casual and relaxed.

'Cool it,' Ruth murmured, feeling that there was something aberrant about this.

'Out!' Milly shouted. 'I shall speak to your foreman.'

'I'm the foreman,' MacPherson said, moving off slowly. Milly gaped at his back. He hadn't closed the door behind him. 'That man's leaving,' she spat. 'I'll speak to Caspar. In the *garden*, in front of us! Can you credit it?'

Caspar came in to tea. The women had returned to the catalogues, Ruth surprised that, after the scene in the kitchen garden, Milly could apply herself to choosing plants. It was as if the sudden explosion of rage had released a load of bile. Caspar listened to her account of the scene in the garden without comment. Milly had no aversion to referring to bodily functions during a meal.

'He's not the foreman,' Caspar said at the end. 'But we do need one on that job. I'll get rid of the fellow; never could stand him anyway: insolent, doesn't know his place. I'll go to Cromack tomorrow and find a competent man to take over.'

Nothing more was said about the riding; Ruth thought it could have been a whim, forgotten in the confrontation with MacPherson. In any event Caspar would have been against it, not wanting his good horse taken to a distant glen and ridden in mountains by a woman who had never been on him before.

MacPherson was sacked the following day, a traumatic experience for Caspar, which was curious considering he'd been unmoved by the image of his urinating before two ladies. Milly came on her husband in mid-morning in the gun-room, pale with anger and downing a large whisky. The fellow had turned nasty, he told her, had threatened to 'get even'.

'There were witnesses?' She was anxious, thinking of the havoc that could be wreaked on the estate by a lout with a grudge, but Caspar had been alone with the man.

'You must find a foreman,' she insisted. 'Someone who'll make sure he keeps away from the camp. We don't want men like that hanging around. You should have a word with Malcolm.'

Caspar's colour was returning but the hand that held the glass shook. She guessed that MacPherson, having nothing to lose, had grossly overstepped the limits. Grimly she recalled how her father dealt with insolence in the days before a servant could take his employer to court with a false charge of unlawful dismissal.

That night there was a second break-in but this time there was no doubt as to how the thief had entered. A window in the kitchen had been smashed (there was glass in the sink) and by the time Malcolm arrived, a hurried search had revealed that a cabinet in the gun-room had been forced and a shotgun taken. It was one of a pair of Purdeys, handed down from Milly's grandfather. Then Caspar discovered that some three hundred pounds was missing from an unlocked cash box in his desk. With some embarrassment he said that he kept such small sums for emergencies. Malcolm guessed that some of the casual labour preferred payment in cash but he wasn't concerned; it was the Purdey that was the problem here. The thief had found the cartridges too, and they weren't kept under lock and key. These people were criminally negligent, Malcolm thought, catching Milly's eye, knowing such carelessness wouldn't have prevailed in her father's time. It was she who told Malcolm about MacPherson and his threat. Malcolm said, 'Didn't you suspect that one of the workmen was responsible for the theft of the painting?'

'It had to be someone who knew his way around.' Caspar glared at the gun cabinet. 'If he came in at a time when we were out, then he could have gone anywhere. We know he was in our bedroom. He could have come down here, but the cabinet was locked: too much trouble at that time.'

'He took a lot of trouble stealing the painting, sir.'

'He thought it was valuable,' Milly reminded them. She frowned. 'There had to be two of them that time.'

'He was friendly with Cummings,' Malcolm said, addressing Caspar. 'When you dismissed MacPherson did he say anything about the painting?'

'No. Not even an insinuation. He wouldn't, would he? Incriminating himself. I mean, when you catch up with him he's going to deny everything.'

'He'll have the Purdey,' Milly pointed out.

'Not among his possessions.' Caspar was wryly amused. 'The fellow's experienced, I shouldn't be surprised if he has a record.' He cocked an eye at Malcolm.

'We'll get Forensics up here, sir; it's possible that he wasn't wearing gloves. In any case he could have left something else behind, like fibres from his clothes.' He drew breath. 'Meanwhile I would suggest that you step up your security' – as if they had *any* security. 'There's a load of expert advice available . . .'

Fleming was summoned and where the CID might have delayed, in view of the Gows' negligence in not installing a security system after the first burglary, this time the detectives came quickly, not because the Purdey was valuable but because it was a weapon. Everyone was hoping it had been stolen for sale or to get even with Caspar by way of his pheasants, but MacPherson was unpredictable, and he was carrying a grievance against the Gows.

Chapter Ten

Two days after the theft of the Purdey Ruth and Charlie lingered at Cougar, airing the house. They had gone there for the eggs and Ruth remarked that the hens should be out of their pen, foraging in the yard in the spring sunshine. Charlie pointed out that, with no one at Cougar, the fox would be cheeky enough to take the birds in broad daylight.

'You ought to be living here,' she told him, regarding the open windows, thinking of the house as animate, responding to the soft air.

'You'd be alone at Camlet.'

She turned and opened the garden gate to emerge on the track. This wasn't surfaced but river cobbles had been put down as a kind of natural hard core and in places the soil was still damp from the thaw. She looked up the track. 'Archy can't be cutting peats yet,' she murmured. There were old peat banks beyond a place called Larach but peats weren't cut until the summer.

'No one goes to Larach in winter,' Charlie said, coming to stand beside her and consider the odd tyre imprint between stones.

'I thought Larach meant "ruin".'

'It does. There's an Iron Age settlement, and the farm would have been named for that. It's a lovely place: ancient oak woods and pastures: an oasis in the wilderness. You'll have to see it in springtime.'

'It's spring now, Charlie. Let's go; we could do with a good walk.'

It was a glorious morning. There would be frosts to come, even more snow, but today larks rose, pealing, into still blue air, curlews bubbled away across the burn, lapwings tumbled, and the track was bordered by yellow bands of celandines. Occasionally they came on the marks of tyres which hadn't been made by a Land Rover nor by Archy's farm bike.

'Tourists.' Ruth was dismissive. 'Or bird watchers.' She was, if not enjoying herself, lost in this fresh world that smelled of life and growing things. Charlie, without betraying his watchfulness, was aware of her interest in her surroundings and thought that, at least for a while, she had forgotten the terrible winter.

They rounded a heathery knoll and, a mile ahead, there was a splash of green below brown slopes and a couple of buildings, from this distance appearing occupied but with no animals in the fields. Blair would put cattle and sheep up here as soon as there was enough grass. Away to the left there were glimpses of a metalled road that looped down across moorland and through the park to the castle.

As they approached it was obvious that there was no glass in the windows of the house, and a number of slates were missing revealing bare rafters. The barn roof was of corrugated iron, one sheet partially lifted, cater-cornered to the sky. 'I bet that makes a hell of a row in a gale,' Ruth said, and shivered.

Crows observed them from a chimney stack, flapping away in silence as they came nearer. There was a distinct smell of fox. 'You can see why I have to keep the hens –' Charlie began, and stopped, his eyes on the ground below the gable-end.

There was a fence in good condition: posts and wire and, sprawled on its back a foot or so inside the fence, was a body.

Ruth stared too long, shook her head as if to settle her vision, and looked away. Charlie had moved forward, stooping to feel the neck. He stood up and, like Ruth, he looked elsewhere, then stepped sideways to squint along the back of the house towards the barn. He came back to her.

'It's MacPherson. His Toyota is behind the barn and the Purdey's under the fence.'

She nodded, staring down across the pastures to the track. 'Of course, it's the Toyota we've been following. He must have come and gone while you were at Camlet.'

'I think he only came here the once, probably a day or two back, even just after the burglary.'

'He was living here?' They were walking along the back of the house and she glanced at the windowless walls in disbelief.

'I doubt it. He's been dead a while.'

'How do you know?' She sounded petulant: shock emerging. 'He'd be cold after a few hours.'

'The crows and the fox.'

Her face went blank, then she gulped and closed her eyes; this death revived memories of the other.

Charlie started to talk, sounding like a lecturer, anything to distract her: 'It's the classic accident that every beginner is warned against: walking with a loaded gun, leaning it against the wire as you step over a fence: a stumble, weight on the wire, gun slides sideways . . . He took the charge full in the throat,' he added brutally, deliberately trying to shake her, to draw her back from the past. He took her hand. 'Let's see what the Toyota can tell us.'

The front of the car was unlocked. There was a tacky sleeping bag on the back seat and cushions which looked as if they'd been found in a skip. There was a hard hat, a pair of workmen's boots, a fluorescent yellow waterproof and a half-bottle of Bell's, almost empty.

'He hadn't spent the cash then.' Charlie held up the bottle.

'He wouldn't.' Ruth gamely tried to play up to the diversion he was offering. 'It would attract attention if he bought a bottle locally, suddenly coming into money. The cash will be in the boot.' But the boot was locked. The keys were in the ignition but Charlie was reluctant to handle them. Afterwards he was to wonder why.

'What was he doing up here?' Ruth asked. 'He'd got the Purdey and the cash. Why didn't he leave the area immediately?'

'Because he was after Caspar's pheasants.' They looked around. This wasn't pheasant country. 'The grouse?' But you don't shoot grouse without beaters. 'He was probably looking for a hare for the pot,' Charlie said, and thought that even if there were a camping stove in the boot, it would take forever to cook a hare. He shrugged. 'We have to report it, and then we should go to Blair and let them know that they don't have to worry about MacPherson any longer.'

Milly was sowing marjoram in one of the greenhouses. She was shocked and then puzzled to hear that MacPherson had shot himself – or rather, Ruth amended quickly because that had sounded like suicide, it had happened by accident: the loaded gun slipping as he was climbing over a fence.

'What a strange thing to happen though,' Milly mused, smoothing soil with delicate fingers.

'Charlie says it's not unheard-of: among careless chaps and novices.'

'But he wasn't – he was a criminal, Ruth! Malcolm told us he has a record of convictions: burglaries and even armed robbery – with a gun. The man would be accustomed to firearms.'

'But if he was used to handling them he'd never have done such a stupid thing as –'

'Ah, but he might.' Milly was thoughtful. 'Criminals use pistols. Small arms, not shotguns. You know, I'm glad; that man was vicious. When Caspar came in after sacking him, he looked quite sick. He didn't tell me what was said but you know how brazen the fellow was. I think he frightened Caspar, and I'm relieved that he's not around any longer. Why, he could have set the woods on fire! Armed, he could have done worse; he could have come back for Caspar, had you thought of that?'

Charlie found Caspar in the birch wood planning a nature trail with Lamont. They were astounded to hear the news although both recovered quickly, Lamont shaking his head in disapproval of such blatant carelessness, looking along the line of posts marking the trail as if this were more important than the death of an incompetent thief. Caspar, in a tone of anxious fury, asked if the Purdey were damaged. Typical, thought Charlie, and qualified it immediately; it was typical of this man in shock. Evidently Caspar was aware of a blunder, adding quickly, 'Can't pretend I'm sorry, you know; he was always highly unsatisfactory.'

'Casual labour,' Lamont growled.

'Yes, well, you have to take what you can get these days.'

Lamont walked away with his bundle of posts. Caspar moved after him with the sledgehammer.

'You've got your gun back,' Charlie said brightly, moving after him.

'And the cash?' Caspar stopped and eyed him doubtfully.

'We didn't root around inside the car, and the boot's locked.'

Caspar nodded. 'He wouldn't have had time to spend it, not if you say he's been dead a while. Crows got him, did they? That's nasty.'

The police were surprised and relieved: surprised that the man had hung around after the burglary, but since he'd been dead for some time, hanging around hadn't been a voluntary act. There was relief that the Purdey had been recovered (one barrel fired) and even the cash which, contrary to Ruth's assertion, had been found in the bottom of the sleeping bag. It was assumed that the man had gone up to Larach as somewhere well away from public roads where he could spend the night, sleeping in the car. He'd gone out with the gun as soon as he arrived; whether unable to resist playing with such a superb piece of craftsmanship or thinking to pot a rabbit was immaterial. Who cared. He was one villain the less.

Ruth and Charlie, deflated, at a loose end, went back to Camlet. Drinking tea on a bench outside the front door Charlie regarded the turned earth in the vegetable plot. 'Soil's warming up,' he remarked. 'Won't be long before we start planting.'

Ruth had been leaning back, eyes closed, absorbing the sunshine. For a moment she said nothing then she turned and stared at the bare soil. She shook her head. 'I've no enthusiasm. I can't grow food just to eat it myself.'

'You can come and work in my garden.'

'You're a better gardener than me.'

'We'd expand: keep goats, ducks, geese; feed the village with organic produce.' No response. 'We could travel.'

She sighed. 'I appreciate what you're trying to do but becoming an organic smallholder or a tourist are only substitutes. They can't fill the gap. Or rather, it's like an amputation; how do you recover the missing part? Everything's changed, Charlie, I'm a different person.'

'Of course you are, so we start over, live differently.'

He detected a shrug and was suddenly firm. 'Right then, you're not interested in this garden and you've no interest in the house. It's not yours. On the other hand I love my home and shortly I must get back to the garden. Why don't we reverse roles and I go home to Cougar and you come and visit? All day if you want.'

That was sly, reminding her that during the nights she'd be alone at Camlet, evenings too. It was the long and lonely evenings that would be the greatest trial for her.

She nodded slowly as if agreeing, not with him, but with her thoughts. 'I'm not staying here.' He held his breath. 'I couldn't take another winter – and what's the point of staying on?' She smiled sadly. 'You want me to move in with you?'

'Do you have to ask?'

'I said "move in" not "marry". Because, you see, it might not work. I may be a thoroughgoing bitch to live with.'

'I'll risk it.'

'Right. I'll set about packing.' He was incredulous – and then he thought that she didn't care either way. 'And I'll have to tell Milly,' she was saying, 'she can do the place up and let it as a holiday cottage.' Her face clenched as if in a spasm of pain.

'What?'

'I must make a start –'

'We both will –'

'I mean, on her room.'

'When you're ready. How about now?' Get it over, he thought, and if it was invasive to suggest that he assist, he didn't want her to be alone in that room where she would see Heather's ghost in every shadow.

The room was untenanted and yet it wasn't, it was redolent of the dead girl. They worked grimly, even methodically, on the principle of give away (Oxfam), throw away (Ruth's face set in stone), retain. At this last she would soften but her voice was steady: 'This we'll keep. Her books are in good nick; they can go with ours.' Despite everything, Charlie relished the plural.

They took the wardrobe first, then the chest with drawers of sweaters, shirts and underwear, Ruth sorting, Charlie packing in cartons and bin bags. Other drawers were left till last, Ruth guessing what she would find, steeling herself further, trying to feel no emotion at the pregnancy kit, the condoms . . .

'She trusted you,' Charlie observed, dropping them in the trash bag.

'But not him,' she pointed out. 'How d'you make out she trusted me?'

'They weren't locked away. And there's her diary.' But that *was* locked.

'The key's in her bag,' Ruth said. 'I guessed what it was but I haven't used it. As for the other things' – she glanced at the trash bag – 'perhaps she wanted me to find them. Did it ever occur to you that we lost a grandchild?'

He wouldn't allow this, and not because he was no blood relation. 'So did Milly and Caspar.' His eyes sharpened. 'What's that?' At the back of the drawer gold gleamed, nestled in lace.

'Handkerchieves handed down – ear-rings – oh!'

She turned to the window. On her palm lay a pair of elegant agate ear-rings, striped in shades of fawn and sepia and ivory.

Ruth backed to the bed and sat down. She looked up at him. 'The dogs didn't bark this time either.' He shook his head, lost. 'When these were stolen,' she expanded. 'How could strangers have entered the castle without disturbing the dogs?'

'It's a huge place – and didn't the dogs know MacPherson?'

'MacPherson? *Randal* gave these to her!'

'Then there were two separate incidents. It was more likely the painting was taken at night –'

'Providing the dogs –'

'But Randal could have taken these at any time.' He came and sat beside her, taking one of the pieces. 'They're rather beautiful, aren't they? Milly will be delighted . . .' They stared at each other.

After a while she said calmly, 'It can't do any harm now. With everything else that's happened, the theft of a pair of ear-rings is trivial.'

'Where did the handkerchief come from?' Milly asked, fingering the lace. 'It's exquisite.'

'They were wrapped in it. It belonged to my grandmother.'

'She treasured them.' Milly laid the ear-rings on a rosewood table and folded the handkerchief meticulously.

'You may like to keep it,' Ruth said.

'No, my dear, that isn't necessary. You don't owe me anything, and we're not responsible for the behaviour of our children.'

'I feel that I am.'

'No more than I. Heather accepted them but I'm sure she didn't know how they were – how they came to be in his possession.'

'Actually she did, but not at first. She mentions him giving them to her but no more; it was after I told her that yours had been stolen and the police were investigating, that she met him and – he – broke it off. That's what she said.' Ruth spoke haltingly and her eyes glazed. 'I'd been thinking –' She stopped. She'd been thinking that Heather had told Randal that she was pregnant and he'd been so terrified he'd fled because he couldn't – or wouldn't face the repercussions. Then she remembered that he hadn't fled, he'd come back.

'They didn't break it off,' Milly said. 'We thought they did but they went on just as before.'

Of course they did, they were happy as larks on Maddy Rigg; the photographs demonstrated that.

'You said Heather mentioned the ear-rings,' Milly went on. 'Is there a diary?'

'Yes. We read it last night. There's nothing we don't know, or haven't discovered since.' No point in acquainting her with the extravagance of Heather's passion for her son.

'The baby?' she asked delicately.

'She refers to the pregnancy.' Ruth winced, then anger replaced pain. 'She was pleased,' she said defiantly.

'I would have been too,' Milly said.

And suddenly, mutely, they acknowledged the bond between them, eyes brimming but restraining their grief, turning blankly to the door as Caspar entered in stocking feet.

'Isabel told me you were here. Something wrong, Ruth?'

She couldn't speak. Milly said flatly, 'She came to return my ear-rings. Heather had them. Randal gave them to her.'

'I don't understand.' It was automatic. He understood, and rationalized. 'Pretty baubles. You never wore them, he'd never seen you wear them. Junk, he'd think. So he gave them away to – to –'

'His lady,' Ruth snapped, unable to bear his special pleading. And there was the painting too, she thought, but didn't say so.

Chapter Eleven

Despite Caspar's objections Milly insisted on reporting the return of the ear-rings to the police. She chose to contact Malcolm because, although it had been Fleming's case, she said the matter was no longer important enough to concern the CID. When she spoke to Malcolm she made no mention of the painting. He thought the lack of curiosity significant and went about his own convoluted way of discovering more. On his next day off he took the private road through Blair's parkland, the one that ended at Larach and which the police used after MacPherson's body was found. Malcolm wasn't interested in the abandoned farm however, his destination was Cougar. He wasn't surprised to find Ruth Ogilvie there; he'd been to Camlet already and found it unoccupied.

Ruth and Charlie were in the garden: Charlie pacing out plots, Ruth businesslike with a clipboard. The sergeant observed them benignly, thinking it looked as if she were moving in. He told them the police were about finished at Larach now, implying he'd just left them clearing up behind him. He didn't mention that he'd been to Camlet. Ruth went indoors to put the kettle on.

Charlie said quickly before she could return: 'Presumably nothing will be done about the ear-rings. She's had enough to deal with.'

Malcolm had been considering this, he was a kindly man. 'She must have discussed it with Mrs Gow,' he said, feeling his way.

'And that was bad enough.'

'Was the painting mentioned?'

Charlie frowned, startled. 'She didn't say . . . We don't dwell on the past: on anything involving –' His eyes jumped.

Ruth was standing at the corner of the house. Malcolm flushed. Her tone was brittle. 'Anything involving what?'

'This isn't official,' Malcolm protested. 'I was just on my way down from Larach' – as if the obvious way down wasn't by way of the metalled road. 'I was only wondering if Mrs Gow mentioned the missing painting.'

'We didn't talk about it.' Ruth was stiff. 'Are you connecting it with the ear-rings?'

Malcolm hesitated. Charlie said, sounding apologetic, 'We did at one time, but now? Certainly Randal took his mother's ear-rings, but he doesn't have to have been responsible for the painting.'

'Fleming realized that the dogs were quiet,' Malcolm told them. 'That struck me too. But a van was needed for that picture, a Land Rover at least, and another man.' He eyed Charlie expectantly.

Ruth said harshly, 'What's it matter? Everyone's dead, Milly got her ear-rings back and the picture's worthless. Why can't you forget about it?'

Light dawned on Charlie. 'They've found the fence!'

Malcolm nodded. 'We found him – in Aberdeen. That is, they found a dealer who admitted it was offered him: a fake *Afterglow* he called it, and he remembered the fellows who brought it in from a Land Rover. And their reaction when he told them it was a fake. So they were on his premises a while and he identified them when he was shown photos. Both fellows have records. They were Jimmie Cummings and MacPherson.'

'You see,' Ruth said. 'Both are dead.'

'That's right.' Malcolm appeared surprised. 'Cummings died in the hit-and-run.' The others made no response but then he hadn't asked a question. 'He was very resentful when the fence told them the painting was a copy,' he emphasized, and waited expectantly.

At last Ruth said coldly, 'The police never found the car that ran him down. Find that and you have your – perpetrator, is it?'

Malcolm's expression was naturally jovial and it didn't change. After a moment he said, 'You got it: perpetrator is the word.'

'He was fishing,' Ruth said when he'd gone. 'Wanted to know if Heather said anything about the painting. They're sure Randal ran Cummings down but there's no proof. He ditched the Mini. Heather told me that bizarre story that she was driving, but that's what he told her to say. Charlie, is it possible he hit Cummings deliberately?'

'Let's think about this. Cummings and MacPherson were only the labourers; they stole the painting for Randal because he thought it was worth a bomb, and Cummings comes back and tells him it's worthless. Did Randal refuse to pay him what had been agreed, and the fellow cut up rough? Threatened to spill the beans? Then Randal came on him drunk in the road and seized his chance to silence him?'

'And he told Heather he'd hit a deer.'

'She must have been terrified when she realized it wasn't a deer.'

'She wasn't, Charlie. Maybe, at first, but don't forget the photos on Maddy Rigg. She adored him. What she thought was an accident didn't change that.'

'It would have changed if she'd known it was deliberate.'

Ideally wounds heal from the inside outwards, closing over new healthy flesh, but occasionally, as with a penetrating stab, the surface grows a mass of proud flesh preventing a deep wound from healing. As time went by it appeared that Ruth and the Gows were healing. Ruth had the advantage in having found Heather and she could be said to be coming to terms with a changed lifestyle. She'd moved to Cougar and she had Charlie. At Blair Milly worked in a kind of frenzy, planning, planting, opening more rooms in the castle but taking on no more labour. She did much of it herself, calling in Archy MacBean to move heavy furniture. She never spoke of Randal to the staff, only to Caspar, and he found mention of his son distressing. Like his wife he appeared obsessed with the business of opening the house and gardens in June. The basic structure of the cascade was completed with the pouring of the concrete and since it was designed purely as an artificial spectacle with shallow, wide steps between turfy slopes, there was no planting to be done. This was confined to the base of the slope where the run-off, artfully channelled, in one place even forming a bog garden, would be lush with marginal plants and aquatics: Milly's department.

Ruth didn't envy the Gows – she had her own distractions – but she admired their industry, however contrived, and hoped they wouldn't lose interest in their projects. Milly had confided to her that she was so tired in the evenings she couldn't wind down or sleep without the aid of whisky. Caspar, she said, always slept like a log.

Ruth had a quieter life, although not literally as Charlie was in the process of erecting a greenhouse against the southern gable-end of Cougar. Meanwhile she explored the neighbourhood, picking wild garlic, nettles and sorrel for the pot, ranging as far as Larach where one afternoon she encountered Archy putting out some cattle. Archy was wearing mountain boots. Ruth, in wellies, had blisters again. Next day she went to Cromack and returned with a rucksack and a pair of Timberland Hikers.

Charlie finished the greenhouse and started walking with her, increasingly aware that there was something behind this activity, as if she were working towards an end, even when she was breaking in her new boots, perhaps particularly then. The way she examined her feet after a walk, satisfied or critical, was the way a rider looks at his horse's feet at the end of a ride. One afternoon in

May he came back from the garden centre to find Archy was visiting. They talked about the weather and the soil, Archy approved the greenhouse and two broods of chicks, and when he'd gone Ruth said with suspect carelessness that he'd offered to take her on the hill.

Charlie hesitated. The obvious retort – why not me? – seemed confrontational. Instead he asked politely where they proposed to go, the pair of them; he was thinking that they hadn't been as circumspect with each other since Heather died – and straight away he had a premonition of what was coming. The wound hadn't healed properly.

'Maddy Rigg,' she said, and it was as if gloves had been removed.

'You're not asking me along?'

'Yes, but to pick us up.'

'I'm to be the chauffeur.' He was angry because he didn't understand this, and she'd arranged it with Archy behind his back.

'I hadn't looked at it that way. It's like this: I'm not a mountaineer but I can cope well enough with the descent. So I thought I'd go up in the lift and walk down' – she hesitated, seeing him stiffen – 'and you'd meet us.'

'I can't get the 'Rover to the shieling.' He was sullen.

'Not the shieling: the bothy to the north, in Glen Carse.'

'You're going to walk from Maddy Rigg to Glen Carse. Do you know how far that is, and a thousand-foot rise at the end?'

'Ten miles, and what's a thousand feet? On a good day, in good visibility, with Archy – who's been all over that ground?'

It had to be said. 'You're going to cover her route. Why?'

'Because she did it.' She studied his face, and saw that he was undecided how to respond. 'Don't say I'm being morbid. Perhaps I am but I need to do it.'

'I don't understand your reasoning. If you were Milly

I could, because she would still be looking – but you?' A flash of comprehension: 'You're looking for Randal?'

'Of course not! He's not my responsibility. Maybe this has to do with getting close to her – like Archy did.'

'He said that?'

'No, he said he went back to find out why it had happened.'

'Why or how?'

'I didn't question it. Sometimes you don't push Archy. He can be rather daunting.' Her tone changed, became firmer. 'If you don't want to do it, I'll call a cab on the mobile as we're coming down.'

'Don't be – Of course I'll do it. And you'll want to be driven to Maddy as well.'

Archy, prompted by Charlie, took no chances, waiting not merely for a perfect day but a good forecast. It was only a short walk but they would take food and extra clothing, and Ruth had the mobile which had belonged to Heather. Charlie had taken Archy aside and told him that if anything went wrong, such as Ruth's spraining an ankle, he was to phone and a helicopter would be there within the hour. But that he, Charlie, would hold Archy responsible, it was all his doing. No, Archy said, Ruth had talked him into it. Charlie didn't believe him, he maintained the idea must have been half and half, and Archy looked uncomfortable.

She hadn't known what to expect, certainly not a sense of familiarity. They walked away from the crowded top station and stopped at the head of a gentle slope of flattish stones and gravel. Immediately ahead was a descending ridge with a couple of rocky knolls, a path skirting the first, climbing the next. There was a steep drop on the left of the ridge, long regular slopes to the right, and the path was obvious, safe, even inviting. The background, to north and west, was one of hazy blue outlines with here and there startling ribands of old snow that gleamed incongruously in the gauzy sunshine. Nowhere was there any sign of cliffs, of danger. The familiarity came with colour and outlines; it was a wider vista of the view from the little hills above Glen Essan.

Archy started down and she followed, crunching gravel underfoot. They came to turf and the path was dusty. She looked back once and the lift was invisible while all sound – of machinery, of tourists – was engulfed by an immense silence.

'Archy!' He stopped. She moved down to him. 'When he was lost, why didn't Randal go uphill? The top station's on the highest point.'

He glanced from her to the summit. 'He wasn't a hillman, any time he was on the hill it'd be with a keeper.' It wasn't an answer.

'How could they have got lost? They took pictures on the top and it wasn't misty. Didn't you see the photographs?'

'I didn't want to.'

'Well, the cloud wasn't down, in fact it was sunny but' – she pointed ahead – 'cloud was coming in from that direction, the mountains were already in shadow. The wind was in the north-west, wasn't it?'

'It got up from that quarter, yes.'

' "Got up"? That's right. It didn't look windy in the photos. Archy, we *are* on their route?'

'Exactly. That's what you wanted.'

'Just making sure. But when did the snow start, and the cloud come down? I mean, they must have been some distance from the top station at that point. Could they have come down here deliberately?' Her jaw dropped. 'Ah! They didn't *mean* to go back by way of the lift! They were walking back to the car. Why didn't anyone think of that?'

'Because of the way she was dressed. Neither of them had any gear –'

She wasn't listening. She rushed on: 'There has to be a

way off this ridge to the left: they meant to loop round to the lift and follow it down to the car park. Even in cloud –'

'No.'

'No?'

'They'd have fallen. You can't see it from here' – he gestured leftwards – 'on that side, all the way down this ridge there are cliffs: one, two, three big corries with great' – he made a circle with his arms – 'like they're enclosed by walls of crags. Anyway, he wasn't aiming for a short cut to the car because the rucksack was on the moor. You'll see when we come to it.'

'The glove came first.'

The glove had been found high on the ridge, in the stones of a cairn. These piles of rocks had been built at salient points but because Archy hadn't been with the rescuers he didn't know which was the relevant one. He knew only that it was some two miles from the summit and on the two-thousand-foot contour but that meant nothing to a man who didn't use maps. Ruth, on the other hand, had been taught to map-read by Charlie and now, producing the sheet from her pack, she worked out that the cairn where the glove had been found could be one at the head of a gully that plunged for hundreds of feet to a corrie. The bed of the gully was a runnel of black slime, its walls at such an angle that even sedums were unable to find a purchase except in cracks.

'Randal could be down there,' she muttered.

He stared at her. 'If he is then she went on alone. Come back from the edge, you're too close.'

She had a wild thought. 'If she hadn't been so happy, she might have pushed him. Did you know she was having his baby?' It hadn't been publicized.

'I heard rumours.' He hated this.

'All the same,' she said, staring down the gully, following her thoughts, 'he could have gone over by accident.' She turned back to him. 'Why did you come out here, day after day?'

'Not here. I came up here the once, right to the top, but mostly I stayed down there, on the moor, looking for him.'

'Why?'

He started walking again. The path narrowed and they had to move in single file. 'Why, Archy?' she called, and then realized that he was deliberately refusing to respond. She continued, pondering, her eyes on her boots. Did he like Randal? The opposite – and you don't look for a man's body if you hate him. Could he have done it for Milly's sake? For Caspar's? She wouldn't ask him again, not directly, but she wondered.

The ridge continued easily with no problems other than the occasional sharp spine which they could avoid by scrambling below it; the sun shone, the ridge ran into moorland and the profound silence was threaded with the trills of curlews and a cacophony of larks. The path was now no more than a sheep trod, masked for long stretches by the heather, but when it was visible it ran towards a flash of green at the head of a glen and the crumbled stones of the shieling.

Archy stopped at two cairns. This was where the rucksack had been found, the rescuers having built the second cairn to mark the spot.

'So either they were making for the shieling,' Ruth said, calculating the distance which was no more than a mile, 'or he intended to veer leftwards and come round under the cliffs to the car park.'

'There's still very rough ground between here and the lift. You'd expect him to go straight down to the road from this point.'

'Perhaps it was dark by then, and snowing, and no lights anywhere –' She saw his stricken face and was seized by compassion. 'My dear! I'm so sorry. Here I'm only thinking of myself and you were out every day –' She checked, he didn't like that subject. 'And Caspar,' she gabbled. 'He was here too, poor Caspar: all that time, searching.'

'He wasn't.'

'What? He was out every day after her – after she was found. Naturally he thought Randal had to be close by.'

'He was never here.'

'Who? What are you saying? Which one wasn't here: Randal or Caspar?'

'Oh, Randal was here. This is – his pack was here, on this spot. But Caspar never came on the moor. Like you said, I was here every day, with my dog. You think I wouldn't have seen Caspar with his two dogs?'

She frowned and looked back at the mountain, then she nodded. 'I know where Caspar went: into those corries you were talking about; he took the dogs and went along the foot of the cliffs. He reckoned Randal fell down a gully – the snow could have given way. And Heather came on alone.' She looked at the cairns. 'With his rucksack,' she said softly. 'Why did Randal have a rucksack, just to go up on the lift?' Archy didn't answer. He was staring across the moor. She followed the direction of his gaze. 'Where was she found?'

He pointed. 'Two miles off.' He went on slowly: 'You reckon they separated at some point and he fell down a gully. The body's caught up somewhere, that's why it hasn't been found by the dogs, and she went off in the opposite direction? That's reasonable, she'd be afraid of the cliffs. It could be. One thing I do know' – he was suddenly defiant – 'she wasn't with him at the end; if they did go on together, he abandoned her.'

'Rubbish!' His anger infected her. 'He pulled her out of the burn.'

He turned on her furiously. 'She died sleeping. She were curled up asleep.'

She had to make allowances, he had no regard for other people's feelings, only Heather's. 'She drowned, Archy. Someone was there and pulled her out of the water, and she wasn't curled up.'

'She didn't drown, she went to sleep –'

'There was water in her lungs.'

He couldn't speak. They both knew he had been blocking it out. Had she done wrong to make him face the truth? 'I can't stand this,' she gasped, 'she was mine as well as yours.'

He put an arm round her shoulders and squeezed. 'Come on, let's get moving. Charlie will be waiting.'

It was a long way to Glen Carse or it seemed like it because this was a pilgrimage and they had to negotiate two sides of a triangle in order to visit the place where the body had been found. When they came to it the burn was shallow and its grassy banks were clumped with primroses. A cairn had been built below an overhanging rock and the rock was some twenty feet from the water. There was no way she could have reached it unaided.

A dipper flew past, whirring downstream like a skimmed stone. There was a scent of thyme and a plover called: an epitaph, Ruth thought; her daughter had died in a beautiful place, and then she remembered that it had been night time, and in a snowstorm, and even without that, beauty would mean nothing to a drowning child. She caught her breath and Archy reached for her hand, so he did care for other people after all.

From this point it was something over three miles to the bothy in Glen Carse. The burn flowed into one considerably larger, the outlet from a loch, and a fishermen's path came up the glen so that only half a mile from where the body was found they were on a good track. They followed it up the bank of the big burn and then forked left to climb to the pass by a path graded for ponies bringing out the carcasses of deer. For all that it was a long climb and they went slowly. Archy told her that this was the way the rescuers had brought her out – he wouldn't say 'the body'. 'The easiest way,' he said. 'In fact –'

'– if she'd known where she was' – Ruth completed it for him – 'she could have crossed the pass and found shelter in the bothy.' Archy said nothing.

They saw the Range Rover from the top; being navy blue it was conspicuous against the grey walls of the bothy. She thought how poignant it was that here on what had turned into a hot day she should be coming down flowery slopes, walking with one friend and towards another who was more than a friend. She stopped and fumbled for a handkerchief, her eyes too blurred to see the ground. Archy turned back.

'What is it?'

She gave a deep sigh. 'I keep forgetting Milly. And Caspar of course. There is some kind of satisfaction to finding the body, to knowing what happened. They don't have that.'

He studied her. She thought she'd confounded him. She always seemed to be doing that. He looked away. 'What are you thinking, Archy?'

'We don't know what happened.'

For a moment she was startled, then she divined his meaning. 'They'll find his body eventually.' She gestured to crags above them. 'It's caught up in a gully over here, or he crawled into a cave and died there.'

Charlie was walking up to meet them, his face schooled until he knew her mood. This wasn't the kind of occasion when one asks the returning walker if she's had a good day.

'No problem,' she told him calmly. 'Archy's a great guide; I can't think how he does it without a map. Knows his ground like a fox.' She regarded them fondly and addressed Charlie: 'Did you have a good day?'

That was safe, mountains and maps were not. Telling her what he'd done in the garden in her absence occupied them until they reached the bothy. Ruth surveyed it curiously: this tiny structure of stones and a tin roof that could have saved a life. The door was wide open.

'Thought I'd air the place a bit,' Charlie explained. 'The blankets would be damp.'

Like most highland bothies not yet subject to vandalism, this one wasn't kept locked, and was thus available as shelter for shepherds or rescue teams, even mountaineers caught out by nightfall or bad weather. Inside there was one room with a couple of camp beds, two pillows and a stack of blankets. Evidently people were expected to use heather or bracken as mattresses. Below a shuttered window was a scarred wooden table, a pack of candles, matches in a screwtop jar, and an oil lamp with a sooty chimney. There was a fireplace with ash in the grate but no indication of what had provided the fuel. It was the barest possible place but it would be sanctuary in a blizzard. Obviously the rescue parties had used it; bare earth outside the door was marked with the imprints of many cleated boots.

They climbed into the Range Rover and as they approached the shooting lodge and the start of the surfaced road Charlie said that they were expected at Blair for drinks. Ruth was surprised, she said she thought the Gows were driving themselves so hard that they were exhausted by the evening. Besides, you wouldn't expect them to be entertaining, in the circumstances.

'Just a drink with neighbours,' Charlie said. 'It was when Milly told Caspar where you'd gone. She called first to ask if I'd go up and give her some advice on her herb garden and I told her I was coming over to Carse to pick you up, and why. She came back later with the invitation, the excuse being to pick my brains about types of herb, but my guess is that they want to know – er – how your trip went. It's understandable.'

'There's nothing to tell them.' Ruth was disgruntled, she felt she needed some breathing space before talking about the day to anyone other than Charlie. In the back of the Range Rover Archy was silent. She wouldn't turn and look at him; she would have liked to read his expression but something held her back, as if an exchange of looks at this moment could carry an air of conspiracy, which was strange because what on earth might they be conspiring about?

Chapter Twelve

From the first moment it was obvious that Milly's mind wasn't on herbs. She took them to the drawing room where Caspar was already at the buffet, alert to start serving drinks, and Milly could scarcely wait until Ruth had sampled her whisky. It was clear from her feverish aspect that this wasn't her first drink of the evening.

'You were with Archy,' she blurted, trying to disguise her eagerness with what appeared to be an innocuous observation.

'We rode the lift to the top and walked down,' Ruth said, hoping it might stay this terse. She had given Charlie the gist of the day's exchanges with Archy and they had agreed to stay together at Blair. He would come to her rescue if necessary although in a large space like the drawing room this could prove difficult if Caspar drew her aside. There was no sign of this yet, Caspar was hanging on her words, such as they were.

'Did you discover anything new?' It was painful to hear the appeal in Milly's voice.

'Nothing.' Ruth's eyes wandered to Caspar. She blinked, visualizing him searching along the foot of those cliffs with the Labradors. She looked round for them but they were absent. 'We didn't take the collie,' she said inanely. 'Dogs aren't allowed on the lift.'

'You mean you might have found something if you'd had the collie,' Milly hazarded. 'But Caspar took our dogs . . .' She shrugged, adding hopelessly: 'It's a huge area.'

Caspar was regarding Ruth fixedly. 'You followed their

route.' It could have been a question, it sounded more like an accusation.

'Exactly, according to Archy. That is' – she checked, swallowed, and continued – 'we followed Heather's. You think they separated, Caspar?'

'Well, of course!' Milly turned to her husband. 'Randal's not there. I mean, with all those searchers . . .'

'Archy says you think he – he says you reckoned . . .' Ruth glanced at Milly and was transfixed by those fervid eyes.

Charlie said levelly, 'They realized you had gone into the southern corries, Caspar. She showed me on the map. It looks likely to me but to them, on the ground, it seemed obvious.'

Caspar looked towards his wife uncertainly. She said, wondering, 'What is this? The southern corries? What's he talking about?'

He spread his hands and turned to Ruth, evidently puzzled. 'We looked down one gully,' she said, 'It was a likely place but the rucksack was found much lower. Although Archy said that even on the moor, if Randal had tried to head directly for the car park, there was rough ground where they could have come to grief. You see, we think – well, me actually – I think it was probable that they never meant to go down by the lift, that they were walking down deliberately.'

'But they didn't have any proper clothing!' Milly protested. 'Heather was in *trainers*. It was winter time, Ruth.'

'Not when they started out. The bad weather moved in later. You know what children are like: think they know it all; if the sun's shining where they are, they don't think ahead.' She looked miserable, and she'd forgotten that Randal wasn't a child.

Caspar said loudly, 'That was my thinking: about those cliffs, the ones higher up –'

'No one mentioned cliffs,' Milly cried. 'You were searching cliffs, Caspar?'

'Along the foot of them.' He was diffident, appealing to Ruth.

'What gave you this idea?' Milly rounded on the other woman as if she were at fault. 'Why bring *cliffs* into it?' Emphasizing the word as if it were alien.

'I don't know that –' Charlie began, to be overridden by Ruth, suddenly incensed: 'Because Caspar didn't search the moors, that's why, and if he wasn't there, where did he go? You see it immediately, when you're there, on the spot. There are four ways off that ridge: down to the shieling or to the road; the way Heather took' – she spat it out – 'or looping round to the ski lift and following it down to the car park – and it was that last way which involved cliffs. Randal isn't on the moors so he's elsewhere, and presumably Caspar had the same idea and acted on it.'

'He didn't tell me,' Milly said sadly, all the fire quenched.

'I didn't want to talk about it,' he told her. 'What good would it have done?' He started round with the whisky bottle 'So,' he said, trying to achieve a lighter note, 'how did you come out?'

'By Glen Carse,' Ruth said, thinking that Charlie had told Milly that on the phone, but memory played tricks after bereavement. 'We came over the pass and down to the bothy.'

Caspar waited to see if she'd say more and when she didn't his eyes softened. 'You've had a hard day. I'm sorry if you found our reaction disturbing. Any news we can pick up, you know?' He was apologizing for both of them.

'I know.' Ruth couldn't look at Milly. She took a gulp of her whisky.

Charlie said brightly, 'Now tell me about your herb garden, Milly.'

She wasn't looking at him, didn't seem to have heard him. 'Randal could cope with rough ground,' she said.

'He wasn't a mountaineer,' Caspar pointed out.

She looked at him blankly. 'My father always maintained that walking the moors was more strenuous than climbing the ridges, and Randy loved going after the deer.'

'Then why –' Ruth began, and stopped.

Milly pounced. 'Why what? Finish it, Ruth.' She smiled, a mirthless rictus. 'Nothing can hurt more than it has.'

Caspar was obviously unhappy about the turn in the conversation but his wife's demands were what counted here – and, Ruth thought, I have suffered too. 'Nothing much,' she said, for all that, trying to lessen the impact. 'It's just that I've been thinking of them as a couple of novices but –' No, she couldn't go on, she'd been about to apportion blame.

Milly followed her without trouble. 'He knew what he was doing?' she suggested. 'You're wrong, Ruth. In good weather he would have been fine; he – they'd have had no more trouble than you did today. He took precautions; he had spare clothing.' Had she forgotten she'd said they were ill equipped? 'I'm sure he had a map and – and –'

'A compass,' Charlie said. 'They go together: map and compass. Nothing's been found. Presumably they're still with him.' He checked in his turn, aware that he was presenting an hypothesis to them as if they were strangers rather than the man's parents.

'Post-mortems are counter-productive,' Caspar said pompously, and Charlie, concentrating on his drink as he restrained an hysterical giggle, heard Ruth ask coolly, 'Have you advertised Camlet yet?' Politely, if somewhat stiffly, they started to discuss the modifications needed to bring Camlet up to the standard of a holiday cottage.

They said nothing on the short drive to Cougar where Ruth collapsed in an easy chair and pleaded for tea. 'I'm dehydrated after all that sun today. Why did we go to Blair?'

Charlie, filling the kettle, accepted that this wasn't rhetorical. 'They needed to know if you'd discovered anything. It was the first question Milly asked.'

'It wasn't.' Despite her fatigue Ruth felt herself in that ephemeral state of mind where, after a drink or two, one is acutely perceptive. 'She asked me if I'd been with Archy, or rather, she stated it. That's peculiar!' She sat up straight. 'Didn't she ever question Archy? He was on that moor virtually every day.'

'I'm sure she did.'

'He didn't say anything.'

'Well, you know Archy; he's not –'

'Don't say it! Who's normal anyway?'

'You're putting words in my mouth. He isn't predictable. He can be unexpectedly formal. He might think his employers' business is confidential.'

'He had no qualms about telling me that Caspar was never on the moor.' Absently she accepted a mug of tea from him, her eyes distant. 'If Milly had spoken to Archy it would have emerged that he'd never met Caspar on that side of Maddy Rigg.'

'So she questioned Caspar. She had no need to ask Archy if he'd found anything . . .' He tailed off but Ruth refused to be diverted.

'Caspar wasn't on the moor,' she reminded him.

'He lied to her. He says he didn't want to discuss it with her; he had to be thinking that it would be preferable for her to visualize Randal's body on the moor, just fallen asleep like – as Archy maintained Heather did. But if Randal had fallen down the cliffs he could have lived for a while, badly injured. Caspar was shielding Milly from that image.'

He poured a little whisky in his tea and held out the bottle. She shook her head. 'I suppose even experienced climbers can come to grief,' she murmured. 'It made more sense that he should have fallen down a gully than that he got lost. I hadn't realized that he went out after the deer; I knew, but I hadn't made a connection . . . Of course,' she went on thoughtfully, 'he'd know all about the importance of wind direction, that's paramount when you're stalking deer. So why walk into a gale?'

'He didn't. The weather was good when they started down, the wind didn't get up –'

'He could see the bad weather coming; he wasn't blind.'

'He thought he could beat it.'

'I suppose. He miscalculated. The gale came so fast that by the time they reached the moor they must have been fighting it for some time.'

'How on earth do you know that?'

'Because they put warm clothing on or she did, when they reached the moor, and they weren't thinking clearly at that point because they left the camera behind.' She frowned. 'You know, it's so clear what happened when you're right there. It's obvious that someone pulled Heather out of the burn so they must have stayed together until she – until the end. Which means that they went – what – north-west from the point where they abandoned the rucksack, yet Caspar searched for days in the opposite direction.'

'He's thick – but then you had to convince Archy that Heather wasn't alone. He'd thought she was –'

'Wishful thinking – not that she was alone, but that she died in her sleep.' Ruth's eyes closed in anguish.

Charlie tried to stay practical. 'So if Archy could convince himself of that despite evidence to the contrary, and Archy *isn't* thick, then so could Caspar.'

'Except that the reason for Archy's blocking out the truth is that he loved Heather and needed to think of her dying peacefully. Caspar didn't.' She added morosely, 'Rather the contrary, in fact.'

'What makes you say that? Oh, you mean because he knew about the relationship between the two of them.'

'Actually I was thinking of the baby.'

'You said Milly wanted the baby.'

'Did Caspar?'

He blinked at her. 'I see what you're getting at. But we didn't know about it until after she – until afterwards, did we?'

Chapter Thirteen

She had warned him that she might be difficult to live with but Charlie hadn't expected difficulty to manifest itself so soon nor so obviously. However, an optimist by nature, he hoped, simply because it was obvious, that it was a phase, and after all it didn't happen often. Evidently her day on the hill had given her a taste for wandering, but alone; she would take off for hours at a time, returning to tell him where she'd been but not specifically what she'd been doing, except that she came back with bags of herbs, some of which he threw out, others he incorporated in his cooking. She didn't exactly refuse his company on these jaunts but he realized that she chose to go when he had some pressing job on hand. Of course if he needed help she stayed, but otherwise she was off, to come home and tell him of this old ruin she'd stumbled on in Blair's woods, of hut circles beyond Larach not marked on the map, of a pine marten in the oaks at the back of Cougar: 'We'll have to watch out for the chicks,' she said. It was amazing how quickly she was learning country lore.

For much of the time Ruth was indeed alone when she left Cougar but on several occasions she met Archy, and by arrangement. He had bought a mobile so they communicated by phone, and when she came home she lied to Charlie. She was becoming adept at subterfuge; she recognized her own facility and took a grim satisfaction in it. She had learned to plot, to draw up a mental balance sheet and, most importantly, to ignore ethics. And she, who had been most impulsive, could practise patience, but only very occasionally. She waited for three days to catch Hayley Lamont alone when the girl took her midday break in the café near her school but Hayley was never alone. In the end Ruth took an empty chair at the girl's table, feigned surprise to encounter her there, and announced that she'd like a word while glancing at Hayley's companions with a smile that was unmistakably dismissive. Intimidated, they left.

Knowing that her quarry was poised to follow, Ruth said chattily: 'Heather kept a diary.'

Hayley, transfixed, said she knew that.

'So you know about the baby.'

'I didn't *know*.'

'Nor did anyone else until after the pregnancy test.'

Hayley blinked. 'He was going to marry her.' It was defiant.

'She told me.'

'I know she did. She told me –' She checked.

'– everything,' Ruth supplied. 'There's the diary. She wrote about the ear-rings.'

'He didn't steal them! He just borrowed them.' Hayley's eyes widened. Panicked, she was reverting to childhood fibs. 'He was going to put them back.'

'Heather knew that?'

'Oh no – I mean, afterwards. He had to tell after all the fuss, the police and that. She didn't know they were Mrs Gow's.'

'Like the painting,' Ruth murmured, looking out of the window, waiting . . . But Hayley looked too and made no response. 'Not Randal, of course,' Ruth went on. 'That was Cummings and –'

Hayley turned sharply. 'She thought it was a deer! She was asleep. He said it was a deer.'

'She was terrified when she found out.'

'Yes, but she didn't do anything wrong, Mrs Ogilvie.'

'And they made it up afterwards.'

'She was in love with him. And I said: they were going to – She'd be sixteen this summer. She could marry then.'

'She'd still need my permission.'

'Not if they went abroad. She could get married now in Alabama. Or Africa.'

'They planned to elope.' It was a statement but Hayley accepted it as a question.

'You mean that day?' She didn't sound all that surprised. 'I wondered. But if she put that in her diary I'm surprised she left it behind.' Hayley's face lit up. 'She meant you to find it, didn't she? You know, Mrs Ogilvie, she was fond of you really; she said you were more like a big sister – except that you disapproved of Randal, but she knew you'd come round in the end, it was just because you wanted her to take her exams. Before they got married, I mean.'

Despite her intention to trap this child into revealing confidences Ruth was touched to learn that Heather had confided such feelings to her friend, but it was a bitter-sweet reward at this juncture. And unexpected. What she'd expected was something concrete, something that would serve to shape some substance in that shadowy void between the summit of Maddy Rigg and the burn where Heather drowned. And there was another void, which Hayley had done nothing to diminish because Ruth already knew about the fantasy of elopement. Heather had thrown Alabama at her mother herself, had mentioned it in the diary – and Africa, where Randal would find work as a doctor with only three years of medical school behind him. What Ruth needed from Hayley was information that hadn't been recorded in the diary. Even fantasies might serve a purpose because one could deduce the truth from reading between the lines. The *fact* was that Heather had recorded nothing in the diary after the night that Cummings died. If she had left the diary accessible expecting her mother to find it, whatever happened after that night was too intimate to record. Or too dangerous. And yet you always came back to those photographs which showed her happy a few hours before she died, as if she had nothing on her mind other than love. Was it possible that they intended to run away that day? And Maddy Rigg was their farewell to the Highlands? They were bound for – America? Africa? I'm crazy, Ruth thought, Heather had no passport, visas, jabs. Randal would know about jabs, could fix things . . .

'Elope?' Milly gasped. 'You're out of your mind.' She climbed down from the steps as Ruth steadied them. 'After everything we said,' she went on: 'both of us. Caspar told him that no lawyer, however good, could save him. And we didn't know then how far it had gone. Randal did, of course. His career would have been finished, Ruth; no way would he ever have considered eloping.'

'Heather did.'

They were alone in one of the show bedrooms where Milly had been putting the finishing touches to the canopy above a four-poster bed. She was aggrieved as she faced Ruth.

'Young girls have crushes. You said that yourself; why, it was you who told me she had this fantasy of coming here' – a wild look, a wide gesture. 'One day maybe,' she added quickly, not wanting to sound arrogant, 'but at fifteen? Randal assured me it was over, finished.'

'That's what we thought, but they continued to see each other, didn't they?'

Milly sighed. 'Look, Ruth, whatever they planned – or Heather hoped for – didn't happen, so why are you obsessed with trying to discover what could have happened? It's unreasonable, irrational.' Her tone became hostile. 'And I'm afraid his father and I are more concerned with present problems than dwelling on the past.' She paused for breath.

Ruth said quickly, her anger rising, forgetting finesse: 'What did Randal tell you about the hit-and-run accident?'

Milly was pale with anger. 'It was a gallant gesture! He would take the blame but he wouldn't confess.'

'So he told you she was driving.' Ruth wondered why she wasn't surprised.

'She *was* driving.'

'She couldn't drive.'

'He was teaching her.'

Ruth swore and turned away. 'Please . . .' Milly was suddenly remorseful. 'We've all been through hell; and as soon as you start to climb out of this ghastly pit, there's another blow that knocks you down again: it's one shock after another. I'm living in a nightmare world. Surely you can understand?'

Ruth was staring. 'Something else has happened?'

Milly sat on the bed with an air of exhaustion. 'Caspar went to Edinburgh to see to things at the flat: bring back his possessions, pay the rent and so on. There'd been a burglary.'

'In Randal's flat?'

Milly nodded. 'The door had been forced and the place was a mess. Caspar can't tell what's missing but the police say that they – the burglars – were after cash and credit cards, that kind of thing: easily concealed. They left the stereo and television because they couldn't be seen carrying them out through a block of flats.'

'Randal would have his credit cards with him.'

'Oh Ruth, you question everything! As I said, Caspar can't tell what's missing.'

'His passport?'

'Yes.' Milly was defeated. 'His passport's gone. The police say passports are worth a fortune to criminals.'

Their silence was loaded, both knowing that, had elopement involved leaving the country, Randal's passport would have been essential.

The morning after Ruth learned about the burglary at Randal's flat, Charlie remarked that he needed to trim the thorn hedge at the end of the garden and to do some thinning . . . and thanks, he could manage on his own . . .

He went upstairs and in his absence Ruth used the phone. He didn't know she did but he guessed. He was consumed by misery, fighting against the conviction that she was having an affair.

During the morning she worked in the garden, hoeing and thinning salad greens. They lunched on soup and his barley bannocks; he drank elder flower wine but she drank water, saying wine would send her to sleep.

Through a screen of blackthorn he watched her set off, tramping steadily up the track towards Larach. He continued to work in a desultory fashion for a while, his mind in a ferment, trying to convince himself that he had no rights over another human being's life, that to attempt to assert any would be to lose her, but this was countered by the question that, if what she was about had nothing to do with him, couldn't affect him, what need was there to deceive him? Was it possible that she was so unhappy, still in grief, neurotically so, that she had to suffer alone, was sparing him her own anguish? Should he confront her when she returned? She'd lie, she'd already lied. Furiously he threw down his shears, rushed indoors, grabbed the binoculars and plunged up the slope behind the house, going fast in an effort to drive out these demons of doubt and, it had to be admitted, of jealousy.

Once he reached the top of their little hill he looped round towards Larach, knowing when it would come into sight beyond the next spur, all golden with flowering gorse. Using sheep trods he worked his way through head-high thickets to a glade sprinkled with daisies and violets. Below, and less than a mile away, Larach basked in the sunshine, a flash of red glinting in front of the abandoned house.

It was too small for a car. He knew before he focused the glasses that it was a farm bike. He couldn't see them with the naked eye and one part of him was warning that he shouldn't look for them, but the masochist was forced to identify that speck of white in the bracken at the hut circles. Feeling nauseated he found her, and then him.

They were sitting facing each other, a few feet apart, she gesticulating excitedly, Archy, even at this distance, immobile, concentrated on her and what she was saying. Fascinated, not yet daring to be joyful, Charlie watched as intently as a bird watcher observing every move of a rare bird, intrigued by the space between them at the same time that their body language denoted intimacy, of a kind.

There was movement. They were standing, still keeping that delicate distance, even as they walked slowly to the bike, pausing, still deep in conversation.

He heard the bike start and for a moment his mind was blank, anticipating her next action. But she stood back, raised a hand, and Archy was speeding towards the metalled road that led to the castle. Ruth didn't look after him; she started walking, not fast but deliberately towards Cougar. Charlie scrambled to his feet, racked by guilt – he must get back before her – then he slowed down. It didn't matter now; this was the moment of truth.

She was in the vegetable garden, having returned to thinning spring onions. Not far away lay the shears where he'd dropped them. She straightened when she heard him coming down through the oak wood and by the time he entered the garden she was waiting, her eyes going to the binoculars, her lips stretched, not quite smiling.

He'd considered a lie to start with: he'd seen an eagle, had gone out to stalk it. He said, 'I've been to Larach – that is, overlooking it.'

She nodded faintly. 'You had to know sometime.'

'I'm all agog,' he admitted, managing a smile. 'So tell me, what is it about Archy? It isn't his machismo.'

'That's unworthy of you.'

'Just trying to reassure myself – and you. I know he's not your lover.'

'You must have been watching closely. Yes, you had the glasses. You're right: I don't need a lover' – grinning – 'I have one.' The grin was switched off like a light. 'We'd better sit down for this, it needs a bit of explaining.'

They moved to the seat in front of the house. 'Tea afterwards,' she promised. 'This can't wait any longer. I should have told you before but it hasn't been easy . . .' She was diffident.

'It hasn't been easy for me.' He allowed the resentment to show.

She reached for his hand. 'I was afraid to tell you. It's like this: after we were at Carse, Archy and me, we talked about it and, you see, one thing led to another and Archy went back.'

Charlie was wallowing in the warmth of euphoria. She loved him, he could afford to be indulgent. 'OK,' he said kindly, 'Archy went back to the bothy. Why?'

'He thinks there's a mystery about Heather – why she died. That's why he's been haunting the moors, needing to find Randal, thinking the body should provide answers. So he went to look for it on the pass but first he went in the bothy and he's discovered that someone was there.'

'All the world and his wife, love. I was there myself. You were.'

'He thinks it was Randal.'

He sat up, alert. 'How did he work that out? You mean the body's in Glen Carse? He got off the hill?'

'Archy reckons he came over the pass and reached the bothy. You remember there'd been a fire in the grate but no sign of fuel? It's only locals – shepherds, rescue teams, keepers and so on – who use that place, and someone makes sure that fuel is replaced. Archy asked around and found that the last people to use the bothy before the rescuers were keepers in October and they left logs and kindling. When the rescuers were there it was gone.'

'Anyone could have been there.' She took a deep breath. 'All right,' he conceded, 'Randal reached the bothy, had a fire, went on and his body's in Glen Carse. Ruth, what's so earth-shattering? His body's in a different place from where everyone was looking, that's all.'

'No. If he reached the bothy, had a fire, holed up, he recovered. He didn't die in Glen Carse. He got out.'

He gaped at her. 'You're saying he's *alive*?'

'Look what he had to lose! He murdered Cummings –'

'Oh no, you can't –'

'You suggested it yourself: he planned the theft of the painting, Cummings and MacPherson stole it, then blackmailed him. He saw the opportunity to silence Cummings and took it.'

'And MacPherson? He silenced him too?'

'No, that was an accident with a shotgun. Randal would never have come back. There's the other – crime too. Heather: a minor. He could get ten years for that. Everyone thinks him dead, he can't be called to book. He'll be in Africa now. His flat was broken into and his passport's missing. Milly *told* me.'

Charlie laughed. He couldn't help it. 'You and Archy: you've been feeding on each other's imagination. I'm sorry, love' – as she made to protest angrily – 'but how would it sound to a disinterested listener: Malcolm, say? You tell him that Randal, wanted for murder and theft – and more; he works a scam to disappear: presumed to have died of exposure on the hill, escapes to lie low for a while, then fakes a burglary of his own flat in order to get possession of his passport, and now he's safe abroad in some Third World country that doesn't have an extradition treaty with the UK, and where they're not particular about qualifications so he can practise as a doctor with only three years of medical school behind him. What would Malcolm think of that?'

'I'm going to Edinburgh tomorrow.'

'What for?'

'To ask questions. Milly told me that Randal said Heather was driving when Cummings was run down.'

'The bastard!'

'Worse, far worse. If it is a scam think what he's done to his parents: thinking him dead all this time. He's a monster, Charlie, and if he is alive, you and me and Archy are the only people who suspect and, as you said, who'd believe us?'

He was surprised at the inclusion of himself in that, but he was tired. He let it stand.

Chapter Fourteen

Speeding smoothly down the motorway in a Range Rover was soporific with Charlie driving and Ruth's musings wandered disjointed until, unforced, they coalesced. 'She left everything behind,' she murmured. 'Not only her clothes and her cherished possessions but her address book. So she did expect to come home after Maddy Rigg.'

Charlie said nothing until he'd passed a container lorry, then: 'And Randal left his passport behind.'

Ruth said, quiet but firm, 'Randal never intended leaving: not with Heather, I mean.'

He glanced sideways. 'You think he was stringing her along.' It wasn't a question and she didn't respond.

Charlie had refused to let her go to Edinburgh on her own, and because her own 'Rover was too decrepit to risk a two-hundred-mile run, and she wasn't familiar with the Range Rover, she agreed reluctantly to his company. She felt he would put a brake on her actions. But they drove south together and arrived at the house identified from Heather's address book at eleven o'clock on a Friday morning.

It was a tall and beautiful house in Kelvingrove, six storeys high, with a security system and cards opposite all the buttons except the one for the fourth floor. Charlie found a place to park and he waited at the foot of the steps while Ruth pressed each button in turn and, as a last resort, the one that must be connected to the flat that had been Randal's. There was no response from the intercom.

Mid-morning, if the occupants were students, they'd be attending lectures. She looked down at the moment that Charlie stood aside for a striking blonde in regulation denim and carrying bulging bags from Sainsbury. She came up the steps, smiling pleasantly at Ruth, watched alertly by Charlie.

'You are here to see someone?' she asked, the accent delightful, and Scandinavian. Ruth said her daughter had been a friend of Randal Gow.

The blonde's expression was tragic. 'So sad. My fiancé told me. I am visiting him. I am from Sweden and I am called Lena. Is that gentleman . . .' She turned, uncertain about Charlie, uncertain what she should do.

'We've come some distance,' Ruth said. 'We are also friends of his parents, and we thought we might run into Caspar – Mr Gow – collecting his things?'

'Mr Gow was here already. I thought the flat is for rent again. It is locked since the robbers were here. I am not sure of the . . .' She was confused.

'The situation,' Ruth supplied kindly. 'We'll go away then. It was just a whim, you know: to see the house where they – where he lived . . . such beautiful houses.' She was peering past the girl who had opened the door.

'You would like to see inside? And . . .' Lena glanced down at Charlie.

'My husband,' Ruth said. 'Come along, dear, this lady is going to show us the house.'

Charlie's smile was as unctuous as her tone but he mounted the steps, glowering at her behind the Swede's back.

There was an inner door with stained glass panels and a tiled hallway which hadn't been swept for a while, let alone washed. A solid side table was covered with mail, most of it junk, and a bicycle with a child's seat leaned against one wall. Doors led off the hall and there was a stone staircase with a cord carpet, a mahogany rail and wrought iron railings. There was no lift.

They followed the girl to the second floor where she

stopped at a door on the landing and indicated the ascending stairs. 'Go up,' she urged. 'You will see the damage. You do know . . .' She hesitated; had it been a mistake to mention the robbers?

'We know about the burglary.' Charlie was soothing. 'The damage hasn't been repaired then?'

'No. Go and see. Everyone does.' Apparently the aftermath of a burglary served as a visitor attraction.

They climbed more stairs to a door with raw gashes on the jamb. Charlie fingered the wood and spoke quietly. 'If it had been a burglary you'd expect more force would have been used than what's here.'

'He had his key,' Ruth hissed. 'The gashes are just a blind.'

'Would the door have been locked when Caspar arrived?'

'What difference does it make?'

'I don't know. Let's go and have a word with Garbo.'

Her fiancé was a medical student, Lena told them as she served coffee in a cluttered, high-ceilinged room, so he'd known Randal quite well; it had been tragic . . . She paused, evidently remembering that there had been two victims of the tragedy, and if the other one were the daughter of these people . . .

Ruth changed the subject abruptly: 'Were you here when the flat was burgled?'

'Excuse me?'

'Broken into.'

'Ah, no. But I was here when Mr Gow came for his son's things. The burglary was that same morning. Mr Gow was lucky, he missed the robbers – but then they were cowards, they ran away: up the stair.'

Charlie said carefully, 'You were here when Mr Gow came, but not when the robbers were here. I don't follow the timing. Who was in the house when the robbers arrived?'

'No one.' She regarded him as if he were a small child. 'The house was empty,' she emphasized. 'I had gone to do the marketing. They must have been outside, hiding, and they watched me go.' She shivered delicately. 'So I was lucky too. Then they broke in, and Mr Gow came and they heard him coming up the stair and they ran up to the top. They couldn't come down because he'd see them, and he went inside Randal's flat and they ran down – very quietly – and escaped from the house.'

Ruth asked, 'How do you know that the burglary didn't happen –' She saw how, and stopped, but Charlie was ahead of her.

'The people in the flats above had to pass that door and they'd gone out already, right?' He turned to Lena.

'Everyone had left. I was the last to go out.'

'Is this the police thinking?' Ruth asked. 'That the burglary occurred after you went out?'

'Of course, because after I came back Mr Gow knocked at the door and asked to use this telephone. He said he didn't want to use Randal's because he'd put his fingers on it and there had been robbers. He called the police from here.'

'They were cutting it fine,' Charlie observed, turning to Ruth who was staring at the door, visualizing Randal hiding on the top landing while his father entered the flat of a son he thought had died horribly on Maddy Rigg. Charlie said, 'It could be that Mr Gow's unexpected arrival was what stopped the robbers from stealing the television set and the stereo.'

'James – my fiancé said they were after his passport.'

'Letters!' Ruth exclaimed. 'That woman's letters!' Addressing Lena: 'You know about the court case?'

'That was stopped.' The blonde made a dismissive gesture. 'It was . . .' She spread her hands. 'I don't know what you would say in English: spiteful? No, James said she was angry. She was afraid for her family, you know?'

'James knew her?'

'Everyone knows her. She lives across there' – indicating the window where, beyond a canopy of fresh young foliage, reared another grand terrace, honey-coloured in the sun. 'Her partner's big,' Lena told them, smiling. 'Perhaps it was a good thing that Randal was sent down for a term.'

Ruth considered the backs of the other houses, wondering if a whole house were a brothel. If not, what kind of people were the other residents? She asked curiously, 'What's her name? I don't mean her professional one, her real name.'

'Professional?' Lena looked blank. 'I don't understand. She is called Flora; her family name I don't know. Is that what you mean?' A thought struck her. 'It was not a serious matter. James could tell you more. I mean, if your daughter . . .' She threw a despairing glance at Charlie, pleading to be helped out here. Not a very bright girl, one who would always appeal to a man for assistance.

'It's not important,' he told her comfortably. 'My wife's interested in all his contacts. We didn't know many of his friends, you see, and we were curious about the affair with Flora.'

'James said it was nothing: "a storm in a cup" he called it. He liked Randal.'

'I'm sure.' Charlie signalled to Ruth who stood up, murmuring thanks for the hospitality.

They left and walked back to the Range Rover. 'Why didn't the police question how the so-called burglars got past the front door?' Charlie asked.

'Randal had a key for that too.'

They came to the car. He stopped and faced her. He said doubtfully, 'Someone will have suggested that the outer door wasn't quite closed.'

'Or Randal disguised himself and slipped in as a tenant was leaving.'

'That's over the top.'

'I agree. But Randal being alive and coming back to get his passport is logical. He's not the first criminal to stage his own death. You do realize that he had to stay in this country for much longer than we thought.'

'Obviously, he couldn't leave without his passport.'

Charlie foresaw danger looming. 'Ruth, what are we doing here?'

'We're confirming that he's alive.' He didn't deny that but nor did he agree. 'He had the opportunity,' she stressed, 'he devised the means – except that he forgot the passport, and now he's got that. And motivation is obvious: he's a wanted man.'

Charlie said slowly, 'If he'd taken the passport *before* Maddy Rigg, then when the family came to clear the flat, they'd wonder why it was missing. He had to stage the burglary to account for its not being there.'

She thought about it and nodded. 'Everything was premeditated. What a sod! His poor parents.' Her eyes widened. 'Charlie,' she whispered, 'where does Heather fit into all this? She couldn't have been part of it, I can't believe that.'

He was considering, but his thoughts weren't with Heather. 'It was a clever plan,' he muttered. 'Where he slipped up was in misjudging the weather –'

'He didn't misjudge it, he saw the blizzard coming and took a calculated risk. Leaving the rucksack where he did was a ploy, indicating their bodies were out there in one of the southern corries or on the cliffs, when in fact they'd gone in the opposite direction. It was too far for Heather and that's where he did miscalculate. He's responsible for her death.'

'He was reckless, yes; negligent if this is more than a hypothesis, even criminally – where are you going, Ruth?'

She'd started walking deliberately. He caught up with her. 'What do you have in mind now?'

'The brothel.'

'What?'

'Where Flora works. Everybody knows her, so the blonde said. We'll find her. Actually this is a job for you. Lena indicated a house situated about the middle of the next terrace. Start anywhere there and ask for Flora.'

'You're kidding.'

'Watch for a man coming out of a house on his own and ask him if that's where you can find Flora. If it is, I'll join you.'

'Are you suggesting that Randal's come back to her?'

'I wasn't but it's an idea. He specializes in making up after quarrels, remember?' She was grim. 'Whether he's come back or not' – seeing his reluctance – 'we'll learn more about him.'

'As if we didn't know enough,' he muttered, and she knew he was thinking of Randal's telling his mother that Heather had been driving when Cummings was killed.

'Don't approach a large fellow,' she warned. 'Lena said her pimp was big.'

'She said "partner".'

'Same thing. Wait for a small guy.'

The other terrace formed an arc and opposite the houses was a small private park with mature trees and a locked gate. On a patch of dusty earth chequered with sunlight a grey squirrel stripped a peanut. Ruth loitered, watching the street out of the corner of her eye, thankful that she was dressed conservatively in a trouser suit which must distinguish her from a street walker. Charlie was having no luck. He approached a young fellow coming out of one of the houses but he was Asian, most likely a student, and transient. He looked wary on being spoken to by this elderly Scot, while a middle-aged woman walked straight past, acting deaf and blind, as if she were being accosted. A girl came along the pavement pushing a baby buggy loaded with shopping bags, the baby bawling in a tantrum, his mother clearly harassed. Charlie crossed the road to Ruth.

'No one knows her,' he protested. 'Either that or they won't acknowledge her existence.'

'Charlie, you only asked two people, and that woman wouldn't say anything!'

'If we only had a surname.'

'I know, and Flora will be her working name but go and try –'

'You try. It's your idea.'

'You're chicken. Right.' If that was the best he could do she couldn't do worse. She marched across the street to where the young mother was trying to cope with the steps, the buggy, the shopping and the baby. 'Let me,' Ruth ordered, not asking. She collapsed the buggy over bewildered protests, picked up the shopping and climbed the steps, standing back for the girl to precede her into yet another cluttered hallway. Ruth followed, glanced resignedly at the stairs, but the girl was standing at a door – the baby, momentarily silent, on one arm – fumbling for keys in a hip pocket. She unlocked the door and turned to the stranger.

'Which is Flora's flat?' Ruth asked.

The other's attitude hardened. 'What d'you want?'

'You'll be a friend of hers,' Ruth said pleasantly.

Eyes raked her clothes, her handbag, and came back to her face. 'You Social or what? I've had 'em all up to here.'

The baby started to cry. The girl's lips tightened and she backed into the flat. Ruth edged inside, not closing the door. She was ignored as the girl dumped the child in a playpen and retreated through a doorway to busy herself in a small kitchen. Ruth put down the buggy and the shopping, cleared a pile of magazines from a chair and sat down, trusting that an attitude of relaxed patience would convey reassurance.

The room was basically turn-of-the-century with a huge sideboard and integral looking glass, a massive table in the window with three fake Restoration chairs, a television set and a glass-fronted bookcase full of paperbacks and videos. A shabby armchair and a nursing chair stood on either side of a gas fire with a stout guard. There was another door which would lead to the bedroom. Ruth had lived in such places herself and thought it comfortable if cramped.

The girl came back, scooped up the baby and retreated

to the kitchen. 'Close that door,' she called. 'I don't want everyone to hear what you got to say.'

Ruth shut the outer door, wondering if the reason she was accepted despite the hostility was that this girl was accustomed to authority. A single mother on child benefit?

The baby was in a high chair. Ruth leaned against the door jamb and watched as some orange substance was spooned into a gaping maw, putting her in mind of a mother bird and its nestling. The girl looked up.

'So what's wrong now?'

Ruth shifted her weight. 'It's fifteen years since I did that.'

'Why look so angry about it?'

'Not angry. Hurt. I lost my daughter recently.'

'Oh, I'm sorry. How?'

'She died on a mountain. She was with Randal Gow.'

The girl's jaw dropped. Ruth thought hysterically: her gape is bigger than the baby's, weight for weight. His face started to swell with rage, he beat tiny paws on his plastic tray, collected his breath and bawled. Absently his mother pushed a little food at him – he would have choked on more – wiping his eyes with his bib, then his mouth. She said clearly, as if Ruth were deaf: 'Your daughter was the one with – with *him*?'

Ruth nodded. The other studied her. 'Why did you come here? It happened in the mountains, miles away. What I mean is: how can what happened here be connected with your daughter?'

'Randal is the link. I need to talk to Flora to find out what happened. I take it she lives in this house. You *are* a friend of hers?'

'I'm Flora.'

'Jesus!' Ruth looked round the kitchen: a few clean pans, a small fridge, an ancient gas stove.

The girl called Flora smiled without amusement. 'His lawyers warned me. You were expecting a prostitute, right?' Ruth nodded wordlessly. 'So there wasn't a lot of point in me dropping the charges,' Flora resumed, 'because it's come to the same thing in the end – except that my mum never got to know.' She picked up the baby, burping him expertly. 'I'll put him down for a wee while and then we can talk properly.' She checked, gave Ruth a hard stare, then relaxed again. 'Yes, you are who you say you are; that was real when you watched me feeding him. You have a right to know.'

She crossed the living room and opened a door to reveal a double bed with a candlewick spread, a cot, a glimpse of a wardrobe, all echoing the outdated respectability of the rest of the flat. When she returned, she closed the door and sat down. 'I don't know where to start,' she confessed. 'And to tell you the truth I'm bored with repeating it. No one believed me. No, that's not fair, my friends did. So – I was raped and beaten up, I brought charges, they blackmailed me into dropping them – and that's it. What more do you want to know?'

'Randal raped you?'

'He was friendly with my husband. They go – they went to the same pub. My husband brought him home one time to watch a video and drink. He said – Randal said he could bring something that would get rid of my rash.' She displayed a hand. 'It's gone now, cleared up of itself. But Randal came round one evening when Alec was at work – he's a bus driver – and he came in, brought some dermatitis cream, and I gave him a beer because I reckoned I owed him and he was Alec's mate; next thing I know he's telling me he has to see if the rash has spread to other places and well, I guess I'm naive and he acted like he was a doctor, but it wasn't till then that I cottoned on and I just didn't know how to handle it. I tried to stop him but he – he went wild, crazy, like an animal. He ripped my shirt, my pants . . . I didn't hit him, I never got the chance, it was the other way round –' She stopped, obviously affected by the images she'd recalled. Her eyes met Ruth's. 'What did he tell you?'

'I heard a story from his mother; I suspect you know

what it was. The gist of it is that it's his word against yours, am I right?' Flora nodded listlessly. 'Of course his mother would defend him.' Ruth was placating. 'In her version you were, are a – working girl –'

'A tart.'

'The police gave you a hard time?'

'The lawyers actually.'

Ruth stared. 'Whose lawyers?'

'Randal's of course.' She spoke as if reciting: 'I am a prostitute. I wanted more money than had been agreed. I attacked him, he pushed me, defending himself, and I fell against the washstand. We have one with a marble top in the bedroom, and before you ask, he knew it was there because he pushed me in there. William was in his cot too.' Ruth's eyes reflected the girl's outrage. 'I did hit my head on the marble because he threw me on the bed and I jerked sideways. That poor little boy saw it all, the noise woke him. I had to've been knocked out for a bit because I came round and he was – doing it.' Ruth held her hands and they were silent for a while. 'My husband left me afterwards,' Flora resumed. 'He didn't like the police and the lawyers coming round. He was seeing someone else anyway.'

'You're living alone now?'

'No, the guy from up the stair moved in. He said he'd look after me.' She smiled wryly. 'What he meant was that he'd be here if Randal came back, only living in the next street, you see.' She shrugged. 'But now the man's dead –' She halted. 'Randal was seeing your daughter?' She was awestruck. 'But I thought – the TV said –'

'She was fifteen.'

Flora moved in her chair. Ruth had the feeling that the girl wanted to take her in her arms as if she, Ruth, were a stricken child, Flora the adult, but the movement was checked. 'You had it far worse,' the girl said softly. 'All I had was a beating and a load of threats.'

'Who were these lawyers?' Ruth was harsh. 'Randal wouldn't have had the cash to employ them.'

'His family could afford it.'

'You're right; his mother could sell a cottage to pay their fees. What did they say to you?'

'They said I'd lose the case if it came to court, there was no proof of anything. I tore my own clothes, the bruises came from one of my customers. They said I had other men here, which wasn't true but you can't prove something *didn't* happen. And there is Ben – that's my present partner. He's a good man and I love him dearly but there you are, you see: the lawyers said there were more, that it's my word against Randal's – and the publicity would have killed my mother, she's had two strokes.'

'Blackmail,' Ruth said. 'Rich versus – well, not so rich.'

'Poor. Go on, say it. So you know why I'm glad Randal's dead; he was a nasty piece of work and no mistake. How did he die?'

'No one knows. The body hasn't been found.' They stared at each other.

'You're leaving something out,' Flora said heavily.

Ruth shook her head, impatient with herself. 'No, he wouldn't come back, he couldn't be so cruel; his parents have been mourning him ever since – He has to be abroad. Anyway, you stopped being a threat to him when you dropped the charges.' But she glanced at the window uncertainly.

Flora smiled. 'You think I should lock my windows and door at night? I've got my Ben now, remember?' She hesitated, then, 'You're right, he'd never dare come back.'

Chapter Fifteen

Over lunch at the Caledonian Ruth filled him in, and Charlie's initial reaction was to ask if Flora could be believed. Yes, Ruth said, because all the salient points of her account bar one fitted the Gows' version, and the one that didn't fit was the most significant. Milly had lied. Flora was not a prostitute.

'But sex with Randal might have been consensual,' Charlie pointed out.

'No.'

He studied her face and knew she'd brook no argument in this respect, but he'd seen another possibility. 'Milly may not have lied; it could have been Caspar who employed the law firm and he doctored their report out of consideration for her feelings.'

'That's consideration: to tell her Randal beat up a tart?'

'Better that than assaulting a respectable young mother in front of her baby, don't you think?'

'Oh, so it's an occupational hazard for street girls, is it? Being beaten up?'

It took a while to restore her equilibrium. They lingered late in the unfamiliar luxury of a grand hotel, then they shopped and it was evening by the time they came to leave the city. They dined at Blairgowrie and arrived home at midnight to a message from Milly on the answering machine to be sure to call her when they got in.

'I don't want to see her,' Ruth said firmly.

'It's too late to call anyway. Sleep on it and we'll talk about it tomorrow.'

She smiled wryly. 'Nice to have someone else to make the decisions. I did the right thing: coming here.'

He was pleased, but over the last twenty-four hours he had had the feeling that pleasure, even relief, was only a temporary lull in some much wider and unidentifiable situation that was the more threatening because he had no inkling of the origin of the threat, nor indeed of its target. But at least Ruth was safe at Cougar.

It was the end of May, woods and banks drifted with bluebells, wet places spired with orchids in every shade from white to magenta. Next morning Caspar came riding down from Larach on his bay horse, its legs dusted with buttercup pollen, foam on the shining neck. Caspar had been riding hard.

Charlie and Ruth had risen late and were lounging outside the cottage drinking fresh Black Roast from Edinburgh and trying to identify bird songs. They reacted in unison as horse and rider showed at the gate, silently, like an apparition. They were still, wide-eyed like cats, giving nothing away.

'I was about to call,' Ruth said, breaking the tension.

'We got back at midnight,' Charlie contributed, not apologizing. 'No trouble, I hope.'

Curiously, that appeared to faze Caspar. He dismounted and looked round for an adequate hitching post. Ruth had stood up but hesitated on her way indoors.

Charlie said, 'We're too modern; there's no post strong enough.'

'No problem. I'll hold him. Just looked in, you know, as I was passing.'

Ruth continued indoors, carrying their mugs.

'What was that about calling?' Caspar asked.

'There was a message from Milly to phone her when we reached home. You didn't know?'

'It'll be something to do with the Opening: her side of it. It's next week, y'know. Out till midnight? Where d'you find to eat till then?'

'Blairgowrie.'

'The devil you did! You went all the way to Blairgowrie to eat?'

'We were in Edinburgh buying an outfit for the Opening.'

'Ah. Aberdeen not good enough for the ladies, eh?'

'Edinburgh's got Italian stuff,' Ruth said, advancing down the path, studying him over the gate. 'For goodness sake, Caspar, put that beast in the yard. The chickens won't mind.'

'I'd rather hold him; he's feeling his oats a bit this morning.'

'He's too fat.'

Charlie stared at her, puzzled.

'I've not had the time to take him out.' Caspar was justifying himself. 'We'll get out more now that the cascade's finished.'

'And working?' Ruth's tone was brittle.

Caspar glanced at the sky. 'There are storms forecast. It's too hot. But that's good; we're going to need plenty of water for the fall, the more the merrier, eh? Fill the burns and the loch, get those waves rolling down. I'm looking forward to it. You seem worried, Ruth. Did I say something?'

She started to speak as the gelding blew impatiently and scraped at the ground. Caspar said angrily, annoyed at his mount's bad manners, 'I won't stay; he's a young beast. Come up for drinks tonight.' He was mounting, the horse pivoting, but Caspar was still agile, he'd found the other stirrup and was in control before the animal could think twice about taking off. 'Changed my mind,' he told them, 'I'm not risking him on the road in this mood; he can work off his high spirits on the hill. We'll expect you this evening then.'

The horse leapt away but was restrained immediately to

a canter. 'You can't help admiring him,' Ruth said: 'able to control an animal with all that power.'

'You were needling him.'

'And he was trying to find out where we were yesterday and what we were doing.'

'I admit, you couldn't call Caspar subtle. Do you think he suspects?'

'But Charlie, what would he be suspecting? He doesn't know that Randal's alive –'

'Nor do you.' It brought her up short. Charlie went on: 'It's possible that if Caspar were merely being inquisitive –'

'He came here deliberately! He wasn't "just passing".'

'– not merely inquisitive, then he could be feeling guilty about those people who intimidated Flora, and wondering if you found her. He must have employed them –'

'Or Milly did.'

'Or they could both be involved.'

'I'll call Milly.'

'Last night you were against it.'

'I was dog-tired. This encounter' – she gestured up the track – 'was a charge of adrenalin. I liked Flora; it was the young mother bit: the baby. I have the feeling Caspar wouldn't have been above employing someone to intimidate Heather.'

'Heather?' He was dumbfounded, then: 'Oh, I see! But in that case Milly would never have gone along with it. You said how distressed she was when it was discovered that Heather was pregnant.'

'You're right; there was a baby and Milly accepted that it was Randal's, no doubt about it, and this was her own grandchild. Flora was different; Milly didn't know her, never met her, and since there was trouble she had to blame someone. Naturally it was the girl, so she dreamed up an image of an evil, scheming woman. Randal was innocent. Milly would always believe him innocent if it was possible. It wasn't with Heather, on the other hand the tragedy did cast a kind of aura round the two of them:

star-crossed lovers. Heather isn't my daughter, she's the mother of Milly's grandchild.' She shook her head, remembering how this had started. 'I don't see Caspar having the same attitude,' she said.

Charlie's thoughts continued in similar vein, ending at the question: how did *Ruth* now view the man whom she thought responsible for the deaths of both her child *and* her grandchild?

She phoned Milly who was in a panic over what to wear at the Opening, an event which had now acquired the status of a capital letter. Ruth said that she had bought her outfit yesterday, in Edinburgh; Caspar, she added, had just come past and invited them up for drinks. 'Excellent,' Milly enthused. 'You can tell me where to go in Aberdeen, what to buy. I can't spare the time for Edinburgh. Did you have a pleasant day?'

'I hate shopping.' Ruth reeled off clichés about age and fashion and sizes while her intelligence warned her that there would be a problem if the Gows discovered not only that had she been making inquiries about the burglary at Randal's flat, but that she had met Flora and knew why the girl had dropped the charges. It was still possible of course that Milly didn't know the circumstances, or the details at least; would the people directly involved be solicitors' clerks or street thugs? Or policemen? But that was way over the top: to think that Caspar could suborn police.

'You'd rather not?' Milly asked sharply.

'Sorry, I was reaching for something. You were saying?'

'You could bring it here. I'd love to see it: your outfit.'

'Oh, Milly! Trying on new clothes: too deadly.'

'As you wish.' Coldly. 'What else did you do?'

'In Edinburgh?' The sense of outrage hadn't diminished with time. She'd been inquiring into Randal's actions but she was doing it on behalf of Heather. 'There were things I needed to do,' she said frigidly.

'Did –' It came quickly and was bitten off. 'Such as?' Milly substituted shakily, as if aware that this was going too far, but she couldn't help herself. She too was labouring under a compulsion.

'It had to do with Heather,' Ruth said. 'I'll see you this evening.' She felt a surge of power as she replaced the receiver and turned, to find Charlie in the doorway. 'You heard all that?'

'I came in at the point where you were complaining about buying clothes.'

'They're determined to find out what we were really doing in Edinburgh. That's why they want us there this evening. Do we go? If we do, either we stall or we have to tell them. What excuse can we give for going to Randal's place?' He was silent, searching for an answer. She supplied it herself: 'The truth is we went there because I think Randal's alive, and he went back for his passport. How *can* we suggest to them that he's alive? It's too cruel.'

'We can't. We could say we went there to try to find Flora by way of his neighbours. We can admit to meeting Flora. That puts them on the wrong foot, not us.'

'We weren't in the wrong at Randal's place.'

'You know what I mean: what Flora told you shows Randal in his true . . .' He trailed off.

'Quite. If we stalled, they'd know it, and if we came out with it there'd be the devil to pay. Imagine: admitting you know they employed thugs to blackmail a vulnerable girl who'd been raped and beaten up by their son!'

Charlie threw a glance at the passage that led to the open front door. 'Let's move outside.'

She went without protest, not realizing that he wanted to be somewhere that no one could approach without warning. Stupid, he chided himself, but he felt more secure outside, remembering Caspar's sudden and silent appearance earlier that morning. Drawing her down on the seat he said, 'You're losing your sense of perspective. If the Gows did force Flora to drop charges of assault that's chicken feed compared with the suspicion that Randal's still alive. The police have him down for Cummings' death, and that's a manslaughter charge at least. What matters is Randal being alive – if he is – not his father being guilty of intimidation. Or both his parents,' he added as an afterthought.

'Can't we wriggle out of the invitation? A bad cold? Toothache? Something urgent: you have to run me to Aberdeen – Listen: I can hear an engine. Oh no, not Milly!'

It was Archy MacBean, ostensibly on his way to Larach to look at the cattle. He stopped for coffee and Ruth gave him an account of yesterday's trip. Charlie listened with some resentment; it was obvious that the two of them had conferred at length over the past days, equally obvious that they had little respect for his feelings, they were united in their regard for the dead girl. He could understand and accept his lover's grief but he was daunted by the depth of emotion that showed in Archy's pinched nostrils and small unconscious movements. A sense of power emanated from the man which could have to do with his simplicity; he was like an animal, a large cat: predatory and controlled by its own focused brain. He tried to conjure up the image of a confrontation between Archy and Randal, and failed. No clash of Titans there.

'He's a killer,' Archy said, and Charlie stared.

'Of course he is.' Ruth was impatient. 'The only reason the police aren't looking for anyone else is because they think he died on the mountain.'

'I didn't mean the hit-and-run.'

They regarded each other, Archy stone-faced, Ruth slowly reading his mind, both oblivious of Charlie who was thinking that the animal was malleable and Ruth had exerted undue influence, no doubt unwittingly. As he'd said, they'd worked on each other' s imagination. Negligence might be criminal but killing meant murder, and that had to be intentional.

Ruth addressed Archy. 'It was deliberate?'

'He never meant her to come back. He was killing two birds with one stone. He pretended to die out there because he had to disappear, and she had to die because she knew what he'd done.'

'She was a witness,' Ruth breathed. 'She wasn't asleep when he ran Cummings down, and she knew he did it intentionally?' She shook her head. 'But she'd never have talked; she worshipped the man.'

'She quarrelled with him,' Charlie put in, startling both of them.

'But they made it up,' Ruth countered, recovering from her surprise. 'Don't forget the photos they took on top of Maddy Rigg. She was happy, it was obvious. She'd forgiven him, even for Flora. Heather knew about her; she would have stood by him whatever he'd done.'

'He wasn't to know he could trust her,' Archy said.

'*That's* why the camera was left behind!' Charlie exclaimed. 'Certainly *she* was happy but he – he was devilishly cunning. He took those pictures to demonstrate that here were two people in love – But then what about . . .' He glanced at Ruth.

'He drowned her,' Archy said flatly. 'Then he pulled her out of the burn and arranged it so she looked as if she'd gone to sleep, like people do out there in the cold.'

'He was a medic' – Charlie playing devil's advocate – 'he'd know about water in the lungs.'

'Not necessarily,' Ruth murmured. 'He might not have got that far, or it could have been a mistake. Murderers do make mistakes. But she was wearing his jacket.'

'He could have been carrying more clothes for himself in his rucksack,' Charlie said. 'It was a big pack.' He sounded cool but actually he was appalled at this conversation. They had surmised premeditation but not to this extent. Thinking that such revelations must be unbearable for Ruth, he tried to force a diversion: 'Who killed MacPherson?'

'It was an accident.' Ruth was dismissive. 'The gun slipped.'

'We should tell Malcolm.' Another diversion.

'He wouldn't believe a word of it. Besides, what could

the police do even if we had proof of anything? He's out of reach in some country where there's no extradition treaty with the UK. He can't come back, that's for sure, but would he care about that?'

'Milly would.'

'No, because she doesn't know he's alive!' Ruth considered that. 'Will he get in touch with them eventually, d'you think? Could he trust their discretion? Milly might not be able to restrain herself, might even tell me: drop hints when she's drinking. As for Caspar, he's stupid; he's even more likely to let the cat out of the bag.'

As Charlie had listened speechless to the exchange between her and Archy, now Archy was silent. After a while he stood up and, without a word, let himself out of the gate and mounted his bike. The collie appeared, jumped up and they left, heading for Larach.

Malcolm was earthing up his potatoes. Burly and sweating, in his shirtsleeves he had the appearance of the traditional bobby on his day off and Charlie knew Ruth was right, the police wouldn't believe a word of the story. They'd be polite, patronizing, and dismissive.

'I brought you a bottle of my elderberry wine you wanted to try.' He brandished it.

'That'll be a treat.' The sergeant stepped across the rows and held the green bottle to the light.

'I think it's like a port.' Charlie was diffident. 'Definitely not to be taken with beef. I'm going to try some in a fruit cake sometime.'

'Now what can I give you?' Malcolm mused, looking over his seedlings for an exchange.

'A few of that late crop would be handy when you lift them.' Charlie regarded the potato shoots critically. 'Mine are all earlies.'

'You're lucky they survived the frosts.'

'I had them covered.'

They looked at the sky. 'No more frosts with luck,' Malcolm observed.

'Rain's forecast but it should pass. They need a fine spell for the Opening.'

Malcolm focused on a small cloud. 'The Gows don't want rain on the day.'

The preliminaries were over – and Malcolm knew that Charlie hadn't come visiting to deliver a bottle of home-made wine.

'Did you hear about the break-in at the son's flat?' Charlie asked.

'No!' The surprise appeared genuine.

Charlie was taken aback but then: 'Maybe you wouldn't know, it's a different force. Would Hay have been told? Surely . . .' He pondered while Malcolm waited with seeming patience. 'His father went down there to sort out his belongings,' Charlie explained, 'and it was he who discovered that the place had been broken into.' Still Malcolm said nothing; they were schooled to let you do the talking, Charlie thought. Aloud he said: 'Caspar reported it of course – in Edinburgh.' He regarded the sergeant fixedly. 'Randal's passport was the only thing stolen.' He stopped and now it was he doing the waiting.

Malcolm said, 'You're trying to tell me something.'

'It was premeditated. Someone was watching the flat.' He went on to recount how the person who had removed the passport waited until he thought the house was empty but had then been surprised by Caspar's arrival.

Malcolm asked the obvious question: how did Charlie know this? Charlie told him. He didn't mention Flora. Malcolm asked why he and Ruth had gone to the flat in the first place. Charlie hesitated, considering a lie, well, part-lie: that Ruth wanted to find Flora. He searched for some form of prevarication but what he came out with was: 'Randal could be alive.'

A blackbird was singing in an apple tree. Malcolm's silence was protracted enough that Charlie knew, but with no sense of triumph, that his announcement hadn't come as a shock, at least to this member of the force. 'Did Hay think it could be a scam?' he asked.

Malcolm said heavily, 'It's been done before.'

'But did Randal mean Heather to be part of it, or was she just in the way?'

' "In the way"? How?'

'She was in the car when Cummings was killed.'

The sergeant's eyes shifted and fastened on the blackbird. 'How did that make her in the way?'

'She was a threat, a witness. Besides, she was pregnant by him – at fifteen.'

'You've gone too fast for me, Charlie.'

'I don't think so.'

Malcolm smiled, suddenly avuncular although Charlie was the elder. 'And if Randal was alive where would you think he was at this moment?'

'If he has his passport then I'd suggest some African country. When Heather thought they would go off together she was expecting him to find work with some Third World government, or any dodgy outfit that would welcome a medical student with a smattering of knowledge.'

'And no extradition.'

'Exactly. There is one point: it would break his mother's heart if she suspected.'

'And his father's.'

'Him too, perhaps more so: fathers and sons.'

Malcolm shook his head. 'You don't really think I'd be passing this theory on, do you?'

'Not to the Gows.'

'Ah. You come to me because you guessed Hay wouldn't listen.'

'I came to you with a bottle of wine.' And pieces of a jigsaw, but there was no need to say it.

Chapter Sixteen

Isabel said, 'I don't know why you have to start entertaining before the Opening; you've got enough to do without having people to dinner.'

'Now, Isabel, it's only Charlie and Mrs Ogilvie; it's not like strangers.'

'And her with a cold too.'

'She's perfectly fit – physically, the cold was just an excuse. She admitted it when I went there. She has to get back to leading a normal life.' Milly swallowed painfully. 'We all do.' She lifted a lid from a pan. 'This fish is done; I've time to change while it cools. I'll leave you to do the vinaigrette; use the raspberry vinegar tonight.'

Isabel grunted, despairing of her. The son's body not yet found and here she was giving fancy parties. Wearing herself to the bone, not eating enough to keep a sparrow alive – not like himself; it was the drink, she said, he got hungry when he drank, and Lord knows, they were both getting through enough of that.

Caspar heard tyres scrunch on gravel and was at the open door before the Range Rover stopped. All his attention was on Ruth as she came up the steps, cool in cream linen and rhinestones. 'You're looking very smart,' he told her by way of greeting. 'I'm glad Milly persuaded you to come.'

In the drawing room there were several malts on display including a new one from Arran. Caspar and Charlie talked whisky while Ruth stood at one of the windows and looked down the lawns to the line of the burn marked by the darker green of foliage and splashes of colour. Milly hurried in, breathless.

'The primulas have taken,' Ruth observed. 'You got the timing just right.'

'Come down and see them.' Milly seemed frenetic in her enthusiasm, poised to bear her away. Charlie, scrutinizing a label, stiffened.

'Later, please?' Ruth's apology was at the other end of the scale, subdued. 'We've been in the garden all afternoon and I'm feeling my age. It has to be the weather, the sudden heat . . .'

'Of course.' Milly was contrite. Caspar glowered and picked up his glass.

'One wonders about rain,' Charlie said, and sniffed to disguise a giggle. It wasn't amusing but it was certainly blatant: the way the Gows tried to separate them immediately on arrival, evidently thinking that if Milly failed with Ruth, Caspar stood a chance of succeeding in pumping Charlie. What would they try next? This must be the object of the malts – and the new one to sample; the guests were to be thrown off their guard by means of alcohol. He declined as Caspar, topping up his own glass, waved the bottle towards him.

'I'll go easy; I'm driving.'

'You can go home by way of Larach,' Milly pointed out. 'It's a private road; you can get as drunk as a lord.'

'I'm not sure about that –' Charlie began, to be interrupted by Caspar.

'The Larach road is more hazardous than the highway!' he flung at his wife, exuding whisky fumes. 'No police certainly, but it's a tricky drive: all those nasty drops above the burn, not to speak of the chance of splitting your sump on a rock between Larach and Cougar.'

'Quite.' Charlie was smooth. 'Not a track for motors. That horse of yours is a spirited beast, Caspar.'

He nodded moodily, unconcerned or unable to keep even this stilted conversation going. Ruth returned to the weather which should have particular interest for their hosts. 'They keep forecasting storms. It was sultry this afternoon and I thought I could hear thunder in the south.'

'Storms could miss us.' Caspar pulled back from wherever he'd been. 'We need water for the cascade but the design's for a long series of falls: watery steps, not a flood. Besides, a flood would take away your plants, m'dear.' Turning to his wife.

'Surely you can regulate the flow,' Charlie said.

'There's a sluice-gate. Lamont will be up there, operating it on the day. We've tested it, y'know' – bridling as if he'd been accused of amateurism. 'It'll work fine, you'll see.'

'What's the procedure?' Now that he'd got Caspar going Charlie was not about to drop the subject. 'I understand the slope is dry to begin with, and you open the sluice-gate – when?'

'As soon as possible,' Milly put in. 'We can't hold up the proceedings while we shepherd small children off the slope.'

'We greet the Member,' Caspar announced loftily, having to make the best of it since the closest he'd got to the Queen was a polite letter from the Palace citing previous engagements. Refusing to try his luck with minor royalty he'd opted for the local MP. He listed the other important visitors: the Lord-Lieutenant, the chairman of the Health Board and so on down to the upper echelons in the hospitals and local government selected by Milly. 'Everyone has been warned of the time the cascade will be released,' she told Ruth. 'You know we got Dawn Kennedy?'

Ruth looked blank. 'Film star,' Caspar informed her.

'She was nominated for an Oscar.' Milly was vague. 'She's pretty. We've seen a photograph. We got her through an agency that specializes in this kind of thing. I think she'll do. She's to stand at the top of the cascade and cut a ribbon, and that's the signal for the water to start coming down and open the show.'

'Where are the guests at this moment?' Charlie's eyes glazed as he attempted to visualize the scene.

'The VIPs are at the bottom,' Caspar said proudly. 'Of course it's not a very long cascade, not the length of Chatsworth's, but you get a better view of the whole. It's not ostentatious.' His lip curled as he deprecated Chatsworth's showiness.

Isabel appeared at the door. 'Are we ready to eat?' Milly asked gaily, and both Charlie and Ruth saw the next obstacle: how could they remain with the laborious subject of the Opening throughout a meal? Could they switch to something that didn't involve the son of the house, absent for whatever reason? Ruth, perceptive as ever after a couple of drinks, felt that she was producing such strong vibes that they had to be picked up by Milly.

They dined at a small table, leaving the refectory table bare except for bowls of flowers. At each diner's place was a bowl of marinated mushrooms. Caspar went round the table with a bottle of Rioja, Charlie peering to catch a sight of the label. Caspar's forte was malts and he made no comment on his choice of wine, neither excusing it nor suggesting approval. It wasn't bad: a fair complement to the mushrooms. Ruth said so. Milly said that Caspar had brought it back from Edinburgh, and what did Ruth bring back apart from the new outfit? Such a treat: the gourmet shops in the capital.

'That's Charlie's department,' Ruth said. 'He does the cooking.'

'Charlie!' Milly was suddenly girlish. 'You don't allow Ruth to cook? So where do *you* shop in Edinburgh?'

He stared at her like an idiot. 'I'm hopeless at names. Now, what did we buy? Bamboo shoots, bean sprouts, shiitake, oysters.'

'In May!' Milly was shocked, overdoing it.

'Oyster mushrooms. You have beech woods; there have to be chanterelles.' He turned to Ruth. 'Haven't you found chanterelles?' The Gows were lost, staring blankly. Isabel came in with a loaded tray. Putting it on the sideboard, she moved to take their bowls.

'What are chanterelles?' Milly asked.

'You do have them,' Ruth told her. 'Bright yellow fungi, just like oyster mushrooms.'

Milly laughed. 'I'm out of my depth here. My interest is in gardens, I'm hopeless at wild things.'

'What else did you do in Edinburgh?' Caspar asked, his eyes bulging, adding as if in extenuation: 'You were there all day. You only went to shop?'

'I had an appointment,' Ruth said.

'What kind –'

'With a specialist.'

'Oh, Ruth!' Milly was shaken. 'I'm sorry.'

Mentally Charlie squirmed, silently pleading with Ruth not to push it.

'Nothing serious.' She was cool. 'Just a woman thing. Hardly life-threatening, I assure you.'

'I don't believe it.' Caspar's voice was high.

'Your salmon.' It was an order from Isabel, telling him to get his elbows off the table and give her space to serve. He leaned back, glowering at Ruth. 'You're fit as a flea.' It was an accusation. 'Nothing wrong with you.' He turned on Charlie. 'Is there?'

Charlie looked uncomfortable. 'It's her business.'

'Leave it, dear.' Milly was plainly bothered, observing Ruth calmly serve herself with Russian salad as if the altercation had nothing to do with her. 'I'm sure you wouldn't like your little foibles discussed at table.'

'Like the leek and ham pie,' Isabel growled, dumping a bowl of green salad noisily on the table.

'Like the leek and ham pie,' Milly repeated meaningly.

'For God's sake, forget it!' Caspar shouted.

'You see?' Milly glanced round the table. 'Sauce for the gander. What happened was that two nights ago he ate next day's lunch before coming to bed. I mean, *after* supper.'

Caspar gaped, then covered his mouth. Isabel said slyly, 'And the rest,' and left the room quickly before Milly could come out with a reprimand. In fact, Milly smiled. 'You can't get away with it, my dear; Daddy always said that no one could have a private life with servants around. We don't have servants as such but we do have Isabel – and despite everything I don't know where we'd be without her.'

'A little more private perhaps.' It seemed Caspar had got a grip on himself. He had been resentful, even furious; now his face smoothed out, his eyes became dreamy, he smiled: a fair copy of a mellow host. 'It was a good pie,' he said.

'Not as if we can't afford it,' Milly observed lightly, and Ruth thought how bizarre this party was with one couple thinking their beloved child was a disintegrating corpse on a mountain, the other pair thinking he was a murderer twice over, and alive, and here they were discussing the host's gluttony.

Another bottle of Rioja appeared and she realized that it hadn't happened by magic; Caspar had left the table to fetch it from the sideboard and she hadn't noticed him get up. Why was that? She hadn't been talking. Was she drunk? She looked to Charlie for reassurance but he was engaged with Milly. 'Those are the easy ones,' he was saying. 'You must try lemon basil and oregano and coriander. And you must have a nettle patch; peacocks like nettles.'

'Charlie, we don't keep peacocks.'

'Butterflies, dear: peacock butterflies. Ask Ruth, she's into all that; won't let me cut down the nettles. Actually they're quite good in a carbonade.'

Caspar sat down, absently placing the bottle close to hand. 'You eat *stinging nettles*?'

'They're full of iron.' Ruth went into lecture mode: 'Great if you're anaemic although it doesn't seem to apply to us. You have to be sure they haven't been sprayed of course. You don't spray, Caspar. The best nettles are around Larach; they always grow well where there have been settlements, which has to do with manure, no doubt. All the old buildings on the estate are lush with marvellous nettles.'

Caspar's charm had evaporated. 'You keep away from – you shouldn't go near those old buildings –'

'Oh, I'm sure –' Milly began.

'They're dangerous! Lethal!' Caspar was shouting. 'Rotting floorboards, cellars, beams on the verge of collapse – think of the weight of a slate roof – we're not insured! Tell her, Charlie.'

'You try to stop her.' Charlie was amused but wary.

'Ruth knows the dangers, dear –'

'No, I won't have it – I mean, I daren't risk it! Ruth, see reason; if anything happened to you –'

'That should be Charlie's line.' Ruth was grinning.

'Do you go in dangerous old structures?' Charlie was curious.

She thought about it. 'Which specific buildings do you have in mind, Caspar? I promise I'll avoid them if it worries you.' She was quite serious.

His jaw dropped. 'Did I give that impression? No, no, I was bothered about you doing yourself an injury, you know?' Wild-eyed, he turned to Milly.

'You have to forgive him,' she said. 'With the Opening and everything, suddenly he's become aware of accidents and insurance and liability; the poor old thing's quite paranoid about roofs and floors and bogs and all the other death traps . . .' She faltered and trailed off. Everyone was more or less drunk and now everyone shied away from the words. Death trap. On cue Isabel returned to remove the plates.

Eyeshine gleamed in the Range Rover's headlights as they approached Cougar. 'The fox!' Ruth gasped. 'Could it have got in the hen house? God, the chicks!'

'Don't panic; you're as bad as Caspar. It's Archy's Rory.'

'Archy's not here. There's no bike. Oh, Charlie, Rory's a hen killer?' A figure emerged from the garden. 'Archy? Where's your bike?'

'Round the back. You're home late. I looked in to make

sure you'd shut your birds in secure. That old fox have got a vixen and she's feeding cubs.'

'Lazy animals, why can't they eat rabbits?'

'Your chickens are easier to catch. You'd best shut 'em up well before dusk in future like you done tonight.'

'Come inside,' Charlie said, thinking that the chap had been hanging around for a while, it was now turned ten. Ruth realized it too.

'You've been waiting for us.'

'Not waiting. I called, went away and came back.'

Charlie thought, Now if I was Caspar I'd ask him what he was doing in the interval.

Ruth sat down in the kitchen. She felt exhausted. 'We've been at the castle,' she explained. 'I've had too much to eat and drink and we've had to stonewall them all evening. Caspar was out of his mind; he demanded to know what we'd done in Edinburgh. I said I'd had to see a doctor. He didn't believe me. He said so.'

Archy was silent. Charlie said, 'He's worked up about something, that's for sure. He lost his rag several times.' He was disturbed by Archy's fixed stare. 'Have you noticed anything? Is it Randal, d'you reckon? Shock coming out with the stress of the Opening and all?'

Archy blinked and shook his head. 'What about her?'

'Milly?' Charlie glanced at Ruth. 'She made excuses for him all the way. He was pretty drunk.'

'Drinking's a symptom,' Ruth said, slurring the words. 'Like over-eating. He steals food. It's done for comfort.'

'He can't steal his own food,' Charlie told her. He was thinking that he must get her to bed but was too well mannered to hint that Archy should leave.

'Stealing food?' Archy sounded mystified.

'It was nothing.' Charlie's eyes were on Ruth. 'He ate a pie, takes stuff from the kitchen, gets under Isabel's skin . . . Are you all right, love? How about a cup of tea? Coffee?'

'He warned me off,' she told Archy. 'Insists the old buildings are death traps. Got quite shirty, didn't he, darling?' She sighed. 'I'd go to bed but I haven't the energy to get up the stairs.'

Archy said calmly, 'Then I'll be off . . .' He hesitated as if about to enlarge on that but all he said was goodnight. After a few moments his bike fired and the sound of its engine faded towards Larach.

Charlie couldn't sleep. Beside him Ruth snored lightly but he became increasingly alert. Unwilling to move for fear of waking her to what would surely be a hangover, he lay on his back listening to the night noises, of which there were few. No fox barked, no owl hooted; once a coot gave one startled cry and once a peal of thunder went rolling through distant hills.

At two o'clock, stealthy as a stoat, he eased out of bed and moved to the window. The moon was veiled by high cloud. On the ground the alders along the burn threw vague shadows towards the house. A shadow moved. There was no wind. He blinked. Nothing was in motion out there, it was imagination. Lightning flickered and he counted to fifteen. The thunder was a subdued threat. Three miles away? Behind him there were little animal sounds and the bed creaked. The country darkened and he looked up to see the moon overdrawn by a heavier cloud. He went down to make a pot of tea.

As he waited for the kettle to boil he remembered Archy had never said why he really came to Cougar tonight. Not to see if the hens were secure because he'd come back. And why did he put his bike round the back?

Chapter Seventeen

The first wave of storms missed Glen Essan; a few drops of rain fell, pitting the dust with miniature craters, but the brunt of the weather struck way back in the hills with the kind of deluges that people accustomed to temperate climates call waterspouts. They had little effect on the land but they were followed by more sustained weather. The clouds dropped and for three days it rained. The burns rose, the lochs filled, the moors were saturated. Glen Essan, greatly dependent on tourism, prayed for sun and Milly stalked her domain like a tigress, maintaining that if all else failed, they could expect hordes indoors. Isabel recruited women from the village to bake yet more cakes and canapés.

Caspar was possessed by demonic energy: tearing round the estate in a Land Rover or on his horse: up to the loch to assess the level of the water, in the woods, on the nature trail, everywhere: storming at Milly, snapping at Isabel, consulting with Archy who, suddenly, had assumed the role of factotum, keeping in touch on his mobile, ready and even eager to perform services which Lamont, working to rule, would undertake grudgingly if at all. Archy, simple but willing as a well-trained dog, would do anything. At this fraught time Caspar leaned on him.

At Cougar Charlie pottered in his greenhouse unaware of the stresses and strains outside his immediate world. Ruth, unable to work in the sodden garden, explored. Charlie thought she had been everywhere but she said things changed with incredible speed at this time of year;

if you went back over the same ground after a few hours, buds and flowers had opened in your absence. He warned her to take care, the burns were high. The way she looked at him made him wonder if she didn't care, and of course he shouldn't have reminded her about the danger of water. There were times he thought that the grief was receding stage by stage, other times he felt she'd retrogressed. He turned to his seedlings for comfort.

'I'm thinking that someone is using that old fishing bothy,' Archy told Caspar, who stared at him.

'Which bothy?'

'On the loch above the waterfall.' All the men called the cascade 'the waterfall'.

'Well,' Caspar barked, 'Why didn't you see 'em off, eh?'

'No one inside.' Archy was phlegmatic. 'Window's barred on the outside and the door's padlocked.'

'So what makes you think someone's using it?'

'I've seen Mrs Ogilvie around. She don't clean for me since she went to Cougar.' Archy was expressionless.

'You've seen her where? Doing what?'

'At the bothy. She's been round all the old places. Not that I've seen her; I know her tracks.'

'You said someone's using the bothy.'

'Ay. She can get in.'

'Mrs Ogilvie!'

'Take the bar out from the shutter, climb in. She's nimble. She's not the only one.'

Caspar absorbed this. 'You mean there's someone else?'

'Of course. She meets him there.'

'Mrs *Ogilvie* meets a man in that bothy?' A long pause. 'Who?'

Archy shrugged. 'Not my business. I thought you should know. Could be someone from the village but I don't reckon he's after the birds, nor yet the fish. They're doing no harm far as I can make out. But it's my responsibility, that bothy.'

Caspar didn't deny it, appreciating the man's usefulness, particularly at this time. 'That's all right, Archy, you did well. Leave 'em alone, eh? Nothing to do with us; we've got far more important things on hand. Now, where's the water level in the loch? That's what concerns me, not Mrs Ogilvie's extramarital – her gentleman friends.'

Two days before the Opening the weather started to improve. Blue sky showed in places and at first the air had a bite in it, more like April than June. Ruth, on the Thursday afternoon, came through the woods, drenched to the thighs because the vegetation would take a day to dry out, to reach the fishing hut on the bank of the loch. The door was closed, the padlock hanging from its staple. From a couple of yards away she eyed it warily. The only sound in the green shade behind her was of water: rills talking quietly as the land drained, a soft fall of drops after a current of air ran through the canopy. She thought that if anyone were around she would have heard an engine beforehand, or a horse's hoofs. She considered how she should open the door: tentatively because she was on private property and didn't know what was inside, or brazenly: flinging it open with a shout because she thought she knew the occupant.

The bothy faced the loch – that is, the window was on that side, she was approaching from the back where the door was. She stepped forward and opened it casually as if she owned the place. There was no one inside.

It was comfortable if one's priorities were few. It had a plank floor, solid stone walls, wood-lined, a slate roof, plastered on the inside, supported by rough beams and rafters. There was a camp bed, a table and several folding chairs, one open at the table, the others stacked. There was a sleeping bag on the bed, a two-burner stove on the table connected to a small Calor gas cylinder. Also on the table were a number of cans, a china dinner plate and enamel mug, a knife, fork and dessertspoon and a packet of candles. The cans contained meat, potatoes, vegetables. There were two medium-sized saucepans, up-ended, clean, and a biscuit tin containing sugar, tea, coffee and a screw-top jar of dried milk. There was no electricity or water. At the back of the table was a bottle of The Macallan, half-full. Under it were two empties. If the occupant had drunk from the loch and scoured his utensils there he'd made up for it with a good malt. Suddenly Ruth realized that there was no shutter at the window, and that this man who had left no clue to his identity could return at any time.

She went out, closing the door gently. She stood immobile, looking into the woods. Nothing moved and no birds sang. 'La belle dame,' she thought grimly, and if you're here, Randal, I'll have no mercy either. Someone was here, and who was it likely to be if it wasn't him? And where was he at this moment?

The bothy had been built at the top of a steep slope in which steps had been cut to the water: a mud slope now, the steps shored up with timber. The rain had deepened channels in the slope and these were alive with run-off; even as she watched, clods of wet earth detached themselves and fell into the loch. She looked towards the outlet where the sluice-gate must be at the top of the cascade but the shore was indented here and her view was blocked.

Something glinted beyond the far bank where a plantation of conifers was fringed with hardwoods. A bottle? A plastic feedsack? Too far away to tell – and then, shattering, there came an explosive report, the echoes swallowed in an eruption of pigeons and alarm calls of pheasants and waterfowl. Ruth had hurled herself against the door, trying to flatten her shape, feeling the weathered wood against her palms, knowing it had been a rifle. Had she heard the bullet strike, was she hit? But she was uninjured although her heart was beating like an engine out of control.

She opened the door and stumbled over the sill, ducking

below the level of the window, seeing now that there was a curtain but unwilling to draw it and reveal her location. Nowhere to run from here but at least behind stone walls she was safe from more bullets. She sat on the bed, the door still open, trying to work out what she should do. She remembered the mobile in her pocket. Charlie! She started to dial, then stopped. If she called him and he came – which he would – he'd be a target too. She cancelled, and considered Malcolm. Thinking what she should say in order to summon him, but needing to warn him, she knew what the response would be: 'Someone out after rabbits, Mrs Ogilvie.' She didn't think it likely that Malcolm would credit her with knowing the difference between the report of a rifle and that of a shotgun. She stared at the mobile.

'Don't use it.'

He filled the doorway, the shotgun gleaming in the light from the window, then he moved to the bed, out of the line of sight.

'Archy!' she gasped. 'I was just about to call you. Who was it? Is he here?' Her gesture took in the sleeping bag, the table and its contents. 'How long have you known?'

He was looking round with interest. 'I haven't been inside before; it's always been padlocked and shuttered but I smelled the cooking. You shouldn't be here, it's a trap.'

'You mean as in booby trap?'

He moved to the side of the window from where he could see across the loch. 'I saw something gleam before the shot,' she said, and repeated, 'Who is it?'

He turned. 'A booby trap? Now there's a thought. We have to get out of here. I'll tell you what we'll do: I'm going to fire across the water and hope some of the shot will make it. If he's still there he'll hear it fall through the leaves and he'll know someone else is here besides you. Charlie? Yes, he could think it's Charlie. Meanwhile you leave, keep the bothy between you and that oak there, on the other side, that one in front of the tall pine. I'll catch you up.'

'Where? Come back to Cougar.'
'Not there. We have to talk.'
'So we'll talk in front of Charlie.'
'Not him. Wait for me by that old badger sett.'

'Wood sorrel?' Charlie said. 'What do you propose doing with it?'

'Salad.' Ruth didn't look at him. 'Had a good time?' she asked on a high note.

'Productive. Now that the sun's out the soil will dry in no time. It was like an oven in the greenhouse even with all the windows open. I have to go to town tomorrow and find some blinds or something.' Ruth turned over sorrel leaves and said nothing. 'You were in the woods,' Charlie said to her back. 'You'd be cool.'

She turned. 'How did you know where I was?'

'Wow!' He held up his hands, warding her off. 'Don't be so fierce, love. Wood sorrel? Woods? Don't tell me . . .'

'What? Don't tell you what?'

He studied her. 'You're hiding something. Are you and Archy cooking up a plot?'

'I haven't been – I didn't see Archy! He's working for Caspar.'

'He's always worked at Blair.'

'I mean, he's far too busy – Look, what is this? I come home from a pleasant walk, picking plants and – so on, and you start in to interrogate me as soon as I set foot inside the door! Before, you thought I was having an affair with him . . . You know, I don't see this relationship working out, I'm not sure we shouldn't split up for a while – see how it –'

'Ruth, what the hell are you up to?'

'There you go again –' She stopped with a gasp. 'I'm sorry, I'm all strung out. I need a drink. It's the Opening, it's come too soon – we haven't had time to recover . . .'

Charlie brought glasses and the bottle, thinking that the Opening had nothing to do with either of them, and

Heather's death was three months back. Something was brewing. He was about to ask if she had uncovered some clue to Randal's whereabouts – he'd contacted his mother – but he desisted. Whatever had happened she didn't want him to know. And if it was important enough for her to pick a quarrel in order to stop the questions coming it would appear that he wasn't involved. Now why should she want him to remain in ignorance? Because he would try to stop her if he knew? He sipped his whisky and saw that hers did nothing to relax her; she was tense and – fierce? Angry? No, she was determined.

'What do we do tomorrow?' he asked lightly.

Her eyes came round to him slowly. 'Do? We?'

He was patient. 'I have to go to town to try to find blinds.' He feigned irritation. 'They'll have to be made to measure, but then the greenhouse is sectional: standard. Probably they do accessories; the ventilation isn't adequate in really hot weather. Surely they have blinds to fit, don't you think?'

'I expect so.'

'I'll give them a shout in the morning. If they don't have anything, I'll have to bodge something together myself. Black plastic seems best, nailed to a frame? I could utilize bin bags. Shall you come?'

'Where?'

'To town.'

'When?'

'Tomorrow.' She'd been miles away, she hadn't heard a word. With a younger woman, even one her age, he might have reverted to suspicion of another man. There could be another man here but he was certain of one thing: that steely determination which preoccupied her had nothing to do with sex. Sex wasn't powerful enough.

Chapter Eighteen

At Blair activity became frenetic as it was anticipated that the Opening was going to be a success after all. The sun was shining, the lawns steamed, new buds appeared to replace sodden blooms, and the water level dropped in the burns although they still ran slightly coloured, but water was water and it would sparkle well enough coming down the cascade.

The refreshment marquee was set up in front of the castle, a spool of blue and white ribbon was delivered to be strung across the top of the slope, and Dawn Kennedy's agent, tracked down on the last evening, assured Milly that they would arrive at noon the following day. They were to lunch at Blair, along with the Member and local dignitaries. The ribbon would be cut at two o'clock.

The luncheon was to be cold, except for the starter. There would be champagne of course and Charlie had been persuaded to do his Baked Trout with Avocado. He was doing most of this at home, bringing filled ramekins to Blair in time for a quick blast from the oven at the end. On the morning he arrived looking ghastly to find the kitchen in turmoil, counters cluttered with cold ducks and salad vegetables, Isabel in charge of women from the village whom he felt he should know but was too distrait to identify.

Isabel didn't ask after Ruth which was just as well because Charlie hadn't the strength to lie; he didn't know how he'd managed to produce the starter but he'd tasted the result and it seemed all right . . . At 12.45 p.m. Milly bustled into the kitchen to say that the company would move to the dining room at one o'clock sharp. She looked for Charlie, knowing the trout would take fifteen minutes and checked, aghast.

'Are you all right, my dear?'

'No.' He opened an Aga oven and slipped the trays inside. 'Hangover,' he growled.

'Hair of the dog?' she suggested. 'Come and have some champers.'

'Not now.' He sounded as bad as he looked. 'Ruth has disappeared,' he told her quietly as the women pretended not to listen. 'Bed not slept in, left a note: "Back soon", would you believe?' He tried to smile but his lips trembled.

'Make allowances, Charlie. Probably she's panicked at the thought of all these people.'

'You think so?'

'She'll be back, I assure you.' Milly's mind wasn't on the words. It wasn't important, Ruth had no part to play in the Opening. Her eyes darted about the kitchen, focusing on bowls of salad, mayonnaise, baskets of rolls. Charlie looked at his watch, pulled out a timer and set it.

'Everything under control?' Milly asked Isabel.

'We're fine here.' The woman cast a distracted eye over her assistants. Milly nodded and hurried back to her guests.

'Dear knows we don't want nothing else to go wrong,' Isabel told Charlie, which he thought was odd. Nothing had gone wrong with Ruth surely, or did Isabel think they'd quarrelled and she'd walked out on him?

A mobile was chirping. Isabel dived for her handbag behind a food processor. Charlie thought how singular was the image: a flushed Scottish housewife using a mobile like a teenager. 'Dear God!' she gasped. 'Never! Well, it can't do no harm, can it? Ay, we'll tell him – or her – sometime. No problem, is it? Why d'you phone then, we're run off our feet here –' She pushed the mobile back in her bag. 'It's fell in the loch now,' she told Charlie.

'What has?'

'The old – that's right, you just arrived, you don't know. Some old bothy up the back: it went on fire last night – hooligans, Lamont says, vandals. Now the bank's give way and it's slid into the loch.'

Charlie gaped. 'Were the vandals in it?'

'Who cares?' Isabel started slicing a duck. 'No, I don't really mean that, but if they were in it, it's too late, isn't it?' She forked neat slices on to plates. 'It was kept locked and shuttered,' she said. 'Could have been a lightning strike, Mr Gow thinks. He knows about the fire, not about the bank giving way.'

'We haven't had any lightning for days.'

'No more we have.' She looked up. 'What's important about it? It's only an old bothy, they got no use for it.'

He nodded morosely. 'Just a thought. Can I do anything for you?'

'No, you watch your starters. Morag, your fruit salad's ready?'

Charlie stood aside, out of the way, waiting and longing for his course to be ready so that he could leap in the Range Rover and rush back to Cougar. If she wasn't there, hadn't returned, he was going to find Archy MacBean and force the truth out of him, because he was convinced that whatever Ruth was up to, she wasn't alone in it and – at least as far as he knew – the only man she was involved with, apart from himself, was Archy.

In the drawing room Caspar, haggard and handsome in full Highland dress, was paying court to Dawn Kennedy who, although only a minor star, in the sombre surroundings of the castle shone like a flame in orange and gold shantung. Dark brown hair framed her face and her eyes were green as a cat's. Caspar appeared lost in adulation and they were both punishing the champagne. Milly, returned from the kitchen, plunged back into her duty of entertaining the other guests, regretting that she hadn't brought Charlie with her for support. She needn't have worried, she hadn't stinted the drinks and the company was already mellow; the prettiest girls from the village were acting as waitresses, enjoying the occasion and showing it. Milly's eyes were everywhere and at two minutes to one she saw Isabel in the doorway. Raised eyebrows, a nod, the hostess collected the company and they moved towards the dining room.

In the kitchen Charlie saw the women leave with the last of his ramekins. He tore off his apron and made a dive for the outer door.

The luncheon was a little rushed, but then with so much drink flowing the guests would have been quite content with a buffet meal. The reason why they didn't have more time between eating and the official Opening was that Dawn Kennedy had another afternoon engagement. However, providing the VIPs were not allowed to linger at table and that the Member kept his speech short, providing the star didn't fall down the cascade in her golden heels, providing the cascade *worked*, the rest of the afternoon should be one long leisurely garden party. The sun was brilliant, the flowers a riot, the lawns looked as if they'd been shaved and they were alive with people who had arrived with picnic lunches when the grounds opened at eleven. The nature trail and the gardens were a dream and the atmosphere was one of gaiety and even pride. At last Glen Essan had its own showpiece castle.

At Cougar Charlie was so weakened by relief that it felt like shock, and only Ruth's command of the situation kept him on his feet. He had driven home too fast and in torment, having reached a point where he was associating Ruth with the fire (recalling Caspar's insistence on the dangers inherent in old buildings) – he'd arrived home to find her washing up in the kitchen. He hugged her, unable to restrain a sob.

She would give no explanation other than that she couldn't sleep and since then, throughout the morning she'd been 'around'. Did she know about the bothy?

'What bothy?' She'd been drying a saucepan but now her hands were still.

'The fishing hut above the cascade. It caught fire during the night. Ruth, look at me! Were you there? Did you do it?'

She gasped. 'Of course not! Why should I?' She steadied herself and frowned. 'You're saying it was arson?'

'Caspar said it could be a lightning strike.'

'That's daft, there was no storm last night.'

'I told Isabel that. Lamont called her while I was at Blair; he's saying that the bank's given way since the fire, and the hut – I suppose it has to be a ruin now – it slid into the loch.'

'It could do that. The bank's eroding.'

'You do know the place!'

'I know every old building on the estate.'

'Were you there last night?'

'No.' She returned his gaze calmly. 'I didn't go near it.'

He said, equally direct: 'I'm worried about you and Archy.'

'Don't be. I wouldn't be here if I needed another man – *that* way. There's nothing sexual between me and Archy.'

'There's something.' He was stubborn, moreover he knew he was right. She didn't deny it, merely looked at him, expressionless. 'What is it then?' he asked, unable to help himself.

'What's between us? A bond. It's Heather.'

It was, after all, confirmation of what he'd suspected. 'Then what are you two *doing*?' That I shouldn't be included, he might have added, but didn't.

'*I'm* not doing anything. And what he's up to I don't know. And that's all I can say.' He was sure she was lying, but she went on, 'We have to get changed; the Opening's at two and we'll only just make it.'

* * *

They made it in good time because the proceedings had become highly informal and at two o'clock the distinguished visitors were only starting to straggle down the lawns to the space at the foot of the cascade, or what would shortly be a cascade. Milly, seized by last-minute nerves, moved to Caspar's side and then wondered how to articulate her qualms. What could be wrong? The water had been tested, the ribbon was strung: a pretty blue and white band at the top of the slope – oh God, her hand flew to her mouth – Dawn Kennedy was down here when she should be up there, and she was sharing a riotous joke with the Member, and he should be speaking . . .

'Caspar, get the Kennedy girl up to the ribbon: send someone with – I'll take her – oh, those heels –'

'No panic, my dear; you look after the Member, I'll take charge of Miss Kennedy. You have your mobile –'

'Caspar, you stay here!'

He leaned towards her intimately. 'You, my dear, are the chatelaine; you stay with the real celebrities –'

'Gow, you are not going to the top.' Milly smiled deceptively for the company, her voice a viper's hiss. She held his arm: ostensibly companionable but very firm, looking round. 'Hayley! Come here. Escort Miss Kennedy to the top, where the ribbon is, and give her all the assistance she needs.' She drew the girl aside. 'And if she falls in or anything, you cut that ribbon yourself, d'you hear?'

Hayley wavered between awe and diffidence but as Milly turned to the Member the girl collected her friends and suddenly Dawn Kennedy and her agent were surrounded by a group of teenagers. Laughing, unprotesting and rather drunk, the two women were jostled towards the turfy slope. After a few steps they took off their expensive pumps and bare-footed, slipping, shrieking with glee, they were hustled up the side of the dry water course like queen bees among attendant workers.

'Going well,' Ruth observed as Caspar called for silence and turned to the slope, perhaps wondering how he might quieten the group up there. Suddenly a man appeared on top, sombre against the bright trees behind him: Lamont. Milly, on her mobile, told him to control the children and, incidentally, to supervise the ribbon cutting.

The Member started to speak, Milly backed away, still on the phone, belatedly remembering: 'Lamont! Who's at the sluice-gate?'

'MacBean of course, we're both up here.'

She sighed in relief. 'Himself hadn't told me. Right, you stay with that mob, and keep this line open; I'll give you the signal and you relay it –'

'Everything's under control, mum.'

'Milly's panicking,' Charlie whispered, amused.

'The Member's doing fine,' Ruth whispered back. 'Considering he can hardly stand up. Nice voice though, well-oiled.'

The eulogy ended and there was a ripple of applause which sounded subdued in the open air. Milly's mobile was clapped to her ear. High above, Dawn Kennedy, striking in her pretty gold and orange frock, stepped out and cut the ribbon. Hayley, on cue, extended a hand and drew her back. Below there was dead silence, everyone holding their breath, praying for it to work.

A wide glitter appeared like a blade along the topmost step and at that moment there rang out from speakers mounted in trees the triumphant strains of the hornpipe from Handel's *Water Music*.

The water spread, and fell. There was a pause and a second blade appeared a foot lower and now everyone was clapping and cheering, enthralled as Caspar's Cascade came sparkling down the wide and shallow steps: clear, with only the slightest trace of amber, but some joker had added an object: round and dark like an old-fashioned leather football.

It came trundling slowly down the steps with the water, and it had to be heavy because it was all the flow could do to keep it moving. The clapping died away and, immobile now, people watched fascinated while the music continued to play. The object came to rest six steps from the bottom, six feet up, on a level with the spectators. It faced them with empty eye-sockets: a charred head with bright bared teeth and a hole above the place where an ear should be. The music played on: delicate, insouciant, and utterly heedless.

'What is that?' Caspar breathed, looking round.

Ruth had approached. 'It's a head, Caspar.'

He stared at her. 'You're dead,' he stated, and turned back to the cascade. 'That's not you? Then who – who?'

Ruth looked at him, at the head, at the top of the slope where the group of young girls clustered motionless, staring down. She came back to Caspar. Charlie, beside her, felt that total understanding was only a whisper beyond his reach.

Milly said evenly, 'Go and stop the music, dear.' She turned to her guests with a soft blank face. 'I do apologize. We've known all along of course, and look: he nearly made it home – well, in a sense he did. The storms brought him down.' She turned to Ruth and nodded serenely. 'Now we have closure too.'

They listened to her spellbound. Caspar walked into the water, removed his velvet jacket and folded it round the terrible thing. He came back to face Ruth, holding out his burden as if it were an offering.

She said reprovingly, 'I spared you the sight of my daughter's body. But then I didn't know the truth.'

'You killed my son.'

'No. You shot him, Caspar.'

Chapter Nineteen

'But how did you *know*?' Charlie demanded, back at Cougar.

Ruth was surprised even though she was exhausted. 'Milly knew immediately,' she pointed out. 'Randal had been using the bothy, and the head had been in a fire, and there was the bullet hole in the skull. Caspar said I was dead, meaning I *should* be dead. It was obvious to me: he'd shot Randal thinking he was shooting at me.'

'How could he mistake Randal for you?'

It was a question that had intrigued the police too because news of that exchange between Caspar and Ruth had reached them by way of Malcolm. Everyone had accepted the uniformed sergeant as part of the proceedings, and even when it was realized that plain-clothes men had been in the crowd it didn't seem remarkable at an event liable to attract thieves. Only Charlie wondered if the presence of the CID indicated that the theory of Randal's being alive had been taken seriously and they'd turned up as they do to funerals, on the chance of something happening.

At Hay's careful urging Milly had persuaded Caspar to relinquish his dreadful burden and he was taken to Cromack where, unsolicited, he began to talk, demanding they arrest and charge Ruth who had played what he insisted was a murderous trick on him. Elsewhere in the station Ruth was giving her statement to men who were unfamiliar with the circumstances because Hay was occupied with Caspar and Skene had remained at Blair. She said that Randal had been using the bothy and the day she discovered this someone had shot at her so it didn't surprise her that he should have tried again and shot Randal by mistake.

Back at Blair Skene and Malcolm climbed to the top of the cascade even before Hay left the scene with Caspar. Lamont had shepherded Dawn Kennedy and the girls down the slope, protesting to anyone who would listen that he'd seen the head go by but thought it was some kind of hoax. Archy, found at the top, undecided what to do about the water – whether to close the sluice-gate or wait for orders – Archy said he'd seen something pass him but he thought it was debris and anyway there was nothing he could do about it, the water running too fast, and him needing to watch the sluice and keep the flow regular. He'd seen no sign of any body.

Since the head was charred the police went to the site of the fishing bothy, now a ruin with only the remains of the back wall standing. Malcolm said that the place had been wood-lined and once the fire had started it would have gone up like a bomb.

'Could have been a bomb,' Skene said. 'Bottle of petrol thrown through a window: the killer trying to cover his tracks.'

The beams had lasted longest and then collapsed under the weight of the roof. Most of the slates had slid into the loch along with the walls when the bank collapsed but a few slates were left on the slope, washed clean by a trickle of water, one with a broken edge that was razor sharp.

They looked down at the water where the tumbled stones showed plainly below the surface. 'The body's under that lot.' Skene was disgruntled. 'We'll have to bring in divers. How did he come to be decapitated?'

'Look at the edge on that slate. The roof fell on the body, a broke slate fell on his throat: it'd be heavy and lethal as an axe.' They thought about it. 'He was dead already,' Malcolm went on. 'He was in the fire but dead before it because of the rifle shot.' His eyes glazed. 'A rifle?' he repeated.

'Could have been a shotgun at close range. We'll know soon enough. What happened to the weapon?' Skene stared at the water glumly. 'Probably in there too. They'll find it; if he threw it in from here, it can't be far away.'

Malcolm looked across the loch towards the plantation. Skene followed his gaze. 'He could have shot from there. He'd need to be a marksman.'

'He's a crack shot.'

Skene was pleased. 'And one of his guns will be missing. Open and shut case. But the man's raving – in shock. He's going to retract everything when he comes to his senses. There's no proof he fired if he wore gloves.'

'We've been here before. Remember the theft of the Purdey when MacPherson was found shot?'

Skene said slowly, 'If this' – pointing to the rubble – 'is Randal Gow in there and he's been alive all this time –'

'And his parents knew –'

'Not both of them. Not his mother. Caspar's in shock because he thought his son should be alive. His mother's *not* in shock because she thought all along that her boy was dead.'

At Cromack Caspar talked. He had no reason not to; he had done nothing wrong, he told them tonelessly, until the end and then he'd been tricked. Up till that moment he'd done what any father would do for his son, so why should he need a solicitor?

'What happened to the Mini Cooper?' Hay asked, trying to put some structure into this by starting at the beginning, or at least at the commencement of police involvement.

Caspar didn't turn a hair. 'He put it in a quarry – flooded, of course. You would have found it eventually but by then he would have been abroad, should have been but for that devil. She killed him, you know that?'

'Who are we talking about?'

'The Ogilvie woman.'

'Was Heather Ogilvie with Randal when Cummings was hit?'

'She was driving. She ran him down.' He spoke as if by rote. 'Randy took the blame, got rid of the Mini, said he was driving.'

He hadn't. Hay considered the point and let it go, but the inspector sitting beside him in place of Skene shifted uncomfortably.

'Cummings and MacPherson stole the painting,' Hay stated, as if repeating an acknowledged fact.

'Yes.'

'And the ear-rings.'

'Yes.'

'They entered your bedroom. They passed the ear-rings to your son . . .'

Caspar stared and blinked. 'My boy borrowed them for Heather to wear. At a party. The little bitch kept them.'

'And he borrowed the painting.'

'No, it was his. All to come to him; he would have inherited everything but for that woman –'

'Cummings tried blackmail.'

Caspar snorted in derision. 'And look what happened to him!'

'Then MacPherson took over.'

'Ha! Incompetent even at that. Said Cummings lived after he was run down: named his killer.'

'Heather Ogilvie.' Hay was smooth as a cat.

'No, no –' Caspar stopped dead. The whites of his eyes showed all round the iris and then the lids were lowered.

'No competent blackmailer would agree to meet his victim in an isolated spot like Larach,' Hay said.

'I stipulated it.' Caspar blinked rapidly, not thinking of his words. He rubbed his hands together then clenched them, fingers entwined. 'He was dead when I got there. He'd shot himself climbing over the wire. He'd be alive now if that she-devil hadn't –' Saliva appeared at the corners of his lips. He made to stand uncertainly and the uniformed constable stepped forward. He allowed himself to be eased back in his chair and a halt was called to the proceedings. Hay thought the man had killed MacPherson but he wanted the broad picture first, however much it was distorted. He had four violent deaths here and he needed to get them into perspective before returning to focus on each in turn.

Later Caspar gave his version of the circumstances surrounding Heather's death, significantly referring to her as a nuisance because, he said, she'd insisted on going on the hill with Randal. That cut no ice: the police had already seen her existence as a threat to a man who could have killed Cummings and had impregnated an under-age girl. Caspar was quite frank about his own actions – up to a point; he had driven round to Glen Carse to pick up his son after his walk (he made it sound so *ordinary*) and the only emotion he showed was indignation at the unexpected break in the weather which he seemed to regard as a personal affront. He was worried as he drove into the blizzard and knew a heartfelt relief on finding Randy alive and well by a good fire in the bothy.

'And Heather'?' Hay said quietly. 'She was still out.'

Caspar regarded him speculatively. 'She wasn't meant to die,' he assured Hay. 'She shouldn't have been there.'

'But she was there. Why didn't the two of you go back for her?'

'She was dead!' Caspar caught himself with such a start that it appeared theatrical.

'How could you know that?'

'Because Randy told –' Caspar slumped and looked away. After a moment he stiffened and his eyes came back to Hay.

'He didn't tell me until afterwards! I'd forgotten that.'

The session ended. 'Randal drowned her,' Hay told Skene. 'Either on impulse, like running down Cummings, or because his father told him to get rid of her. The whole trip was premeditated, planned so that Randal should disappear, and Heather was to be eliminated.'

'From what we know of Randal he doesn't seem the kind of guy to murder in cold blood; he was violent but – premeditated?'

'His father would do anything to avoid scandal, and he was calling the shots: providing cash, shelter, know-how; Randal had to do as he was told. And he knew what a risk Heather represented; the way their minds worked, father and son, she could have turned on Randal at any time.'

Next day Caspar, fresh from sleep, avoided the subject of Heather but he did admit that, when everyone thought he was searching for Randal's body, he was in fact finding a flat in St Andrews, and establishing his son in a warren of students' quarters where he could lie low until such time as he could be smuggled out of the country. Caspar kept him supplied with food and other essential items, eventually staging the break-in and entering the rooms in Kelvingrove to obtain the passport. Mention of this reminded him of Ruth and he went into a furious tirade maintaining that she had spied on him, had gone to Kelvingrove and interrogated his son's neighbours, had even found the prostitute who alleged that Randal assaulted her – but had dropped the charges, he added quickly, she didn't have a leg to stand on. The Ogilvie woman had acted suspiciously so Caspar had phoned the neighbour, some foreign girl, who told him that an old country couple (obviously Innes and Ogilvie) had come and questioned her about the tart. When they left she'd watched them walk round to the next street where the woman had her beat. Caspar was beside himself now and he appealed to Hay: wasn't that outrageous, a criminal act?

'So the Ogilvie woman had to go,' Hay concluded for him.

'She was a nuisance, like Heather.'

Caspar shook his head, sadly it seemed. 'He was a poor shot. Well, not poor, just not good enough.'

They were mystified and failed to hide it. 'You thought that was me.' Caspar's voice was normal, even amused.

'I wouldn't have missed. Randy came down to Blair and took – he borrowed the rifle. He could have killed her, you know, but she had a shotgun. Returned his fire.'

'When was this?' Hay asked quickly.

'Do you own a shotgun?'

Ruth was astonished. 'Good Lord no!'

Hay looked at Charlie who shook his head. 'Nor me,' he said. 'Why?'

Hay turned back to Ruth. 'In your statement you're pretty casual about the attempt on your life.'

'You know as much about it as I do.' She was still amazed.

'I'm talking about when you *were* in the bothy and he fired at you.'

Charlie gaped at him, then turned to her. They were in Cougar's kitchen, which Hay had thought more formal, more suited to the occasion than the garden where he'd found them. Skene was in attendance.

'What is this?' Charlie protested. 'Someone fired at you . . .' He tailed off and licked his lips, resolving to keep quiet, at least until he saw what was in the wind.

Ruth was apologetic. 'It was one afternoon. The bothy was unlocked so I went in and, well, someone fired . . . At the time I never thought I was the target; I thought someone was after rabbits, they're all over the banks of the loch.'

'Was it a rifle or a shotgun?'

'Is there a difference?'

Charlie was expressionless, and then remembered to show concern.

'Caspar says Randal fired at you with a rifle,' Hay told her.

Now Charlie was concerned. He said, 'Wouldn't it have been Caspar himself, and now he's trying to shift the blame to a dead man? After all, it was Caspar the second time – I mean, when he thought he was shooting at Ruth.'

Hay ignored him. 'How many shots were fired?' he asked Ruth.

'Only one.'

'He didn't fire again? Or someone else did – like there were two of them, or someone returning his fire?'

She was exasperated. 'No! Look, this is irrelevant; the first time was only an attempt – if it wasn't someone out rabbiting – the second was murder. Or will it be brought in as manslaughter since it was a mistake?'

He ignored the sarcasm. 'The mistake intrigues me. What made Caspar think it was you in the bothy?'

She regarded him thoughtfully, elbows on the table, her chin on her hands. 'We've been wondering about that. I walk all over the estate and he'd warned me to keep away from the old buildings, said they were dangerous. Randal was using the bothy and his father would have taken him food, which would be how he came to see me hanging around on the afternoon he shot at me – since he's told you he did. I suppose he came back after dark, saw a shadow on the curtain, assumed it was me, and fired.'

Hay nodded and rephrased his question. 'What made him assume it was you when, so far as he knew, the bothy was occupied by his son?'

'But it *was* occupied by Randal!' Ruth stared. 'Are you saying Caspar *meant* to shoot him?'

'No, no.' Hay waved it aside, annoyed. 'But there are two points at issue: first, Randal should *not* have been there, and second, you *should* have been. As if Caspar had told Randal to absent himself, and had attempted to lure you to the bothy. What went wrong – from Caspar's point of view?'

She looked blank. 'There was no attempt to "lure" me. The opposite, in fact. He warned me to keep away from the buildings.'

Hay sighed as if defeated. 'No doubt we'll find out in time. But something made him think it was you.'

Ruth shrugged. 'The man's paranoid – mad –' Her eyes glittered but she didn't go on.

'What were you about to say then?' Charlie asked when the police had driven away.

'I was about to question how a deranged man could have planned the second murder.'

'The second?'

'Cummings was the first,' she told him. 'That was a result of Randal acting on impulse, on his own. Then there was Heather. Caspar planned everything: meeting Randal to spirit him away, harbouring him, killing MacPherson for some reason – blackmail no doubt. Caspar was responsible for Heather's death. I know it. That's why he had to die.'

'Caspar isn't dead, Ruth.'

'Worse. Can you imagine what it's like to kill your own son by mistake? And then have to face his mother? Caspar has to live with that: a living death. Think of Milly. What happens to her mind when she realizes Randal was so close to her – alive – for months, and she could have gone to him? She would have forgiven him everything, even convinced herself that Heather's death was an accident. If I was her I'd go –' She didn't finish, thinking that she had suffered and not gone mad.

'Hay has a point,' Charlie said, keeping on safer ground. 'How did that substitution come about: Randal being in the bothy but Caspar thinking his shadow was yours – if it happened that way, which seems the most likely?'

'Don't glower at me.'

'It was the night you didn't come to bed, or you came and then left. Where did you go?'

'I wasn't at the bothy.'

'No, or Caspar would have shot you. But he thought you were there. Ah, you told him you were going to be there!'

'Don't be stupid. He hated me like poison by then. He'd have smelled a trap – a rat – he'd have smelled a rat if I'd told him I was going to the bothy.'

'A trap. That's it. Something told him you were going to be there.'

'With Randal in occupation? Come off it.'

'No. Randal was out of the way. Caspar had told him not to go near the bothy.' She said nothing, watching him. He shook his head. 'That won't do either; if Caspar had told him not to be in the bothy on that particular night Randal would have followed orders, but he didn't. He *was* there but Caspar thought he wasn't . . .' Charlie emerged from his musing to see that Ruth was tense, listening as if she were hearing something else, or words unsaid. 'What?' he asked and, seeing her shift guiltily, he considered what he'd been saying. His eyes narrowed. 'Archy,' he breathed, and suddenly she was again focused on him.

'No post-mortems,' she announced. 'We've had enough of them. As Milly says, we both have closure now.'

'Him too. It was Archy, wasn't it? He'd become Caspar's right-hand man – indispensable, the only person he could trust – and staying close to him meant Archy might be able to forestall him if he intended to harm you. That's why – I never told you but that night Archy was here, ostensibly to see if I'd shut the hens up, I fancied there was someone down by the burn in the small hours. Now I think it was Archy looking out for you, probably not the first time either. Perhaps he knew that Caspar was out that night and he was making sure he didn't come here.' Charlie was seized by amazement. 'Why on earth didn't you tell me?'

She shook her head helplessly. 'I didn't think it was dangerous.'

'Not dangerous! You were fired on! I bet you told Archy.'

She sighed. She didn't want to involve him more than was absolutely necessary. 'He had a stake in it.'

'I didn't?'

'Not like Archy – and me.'

'You said that before.' He was resentful but he came back to his basic contention: 'You knew the bothy was being used by Randal, so Archy had to know as well.

There's a bed? Obviously. So Archy told Caspar – the place was being used – by you . . .' He spoke slowly, working it out, watching her face. 'He said he'd seen you there, he reckoned you met a man – a lover – at night?' His voice climbed.

'How could I go there if Randal was using the place?'

'He wasn't! He had another bolt-hole, or holes, he could have been in an attic at the castle, or a hay-loft, anywhere.'

'But he wasn't, Charlie; he was in the bothy! Caspar shot him there.'

He was silent for a moment, frowning, then his face cleared. 'Archy knew where he'd gone, went to him and told him to meet Caspar at the bothy. Something was to be handed over: cash, airline tickets – a visa? Wouldn't Randal be expecting something like that?'

She said quickly, 'Why use Archy? For heaven's sake, everyone's got mobiles.'

'Calls can be traced. Caspar would never have risked it, probably never let Randal have a mobile after he left his behind in the Escort. And I didn't say Caspar *sent* Archy, he was operating on his own of course.'

'No, Randal was supposed to be dead; how would he trust someone who – knew he was alive – and . . .' She paused, at a loss.

'That's it! Archy had to be trusted *because* he knew so much. By playing the simpleton he could demonstrate that he was completely in Caspar's confidence, and since he knew everything – about the bothy, where to find Randal – the man fell for it. No mobile either, remember, Randal had no way of checking. It had to happen something like that because Randal came to the bothy, didn't he? And Caspar was there, waiting for you. Where were you?'

She'd been at Archy's cottage. He'd said she should keep out of sight until the Opening. She'd known he was planning something but he hadn't told her what it was. She trusted him implicitly and hadn't probed.

'I told you: I went for a walk.'

'At night?'

'No, at dawn. I like to watch the sun rise. You were fast asleep.' She had become a good liar.

Proof had been the problem all along but now, knowing what to look for, the police started to make discoveries, the first being Randal's body under the rubble in the loch. That it was his was certain because it belonged to the head and his teeth had been identified by his dentist. The rifle was in the water too; that took longer to find because it was on the opposite side of the loch where Caspar had thrown it after shooting from the plantation.

Caspar didn't confess as such, he rambled, and while it was being debated whether he was fit to stand trial he took the matter into his own hands by fashioning a rope from strips of blanket and hanging himself from the bar of the ventilator in his cell.

Back in the hills behind Larach hikers found a small green mountain tent containing camping equipment but no camper, and Randal's fingerprints were on everything. As Charlie had surmised, Randal had more than one bolt-hole. He nearly got away with it too but neither of the Gow men was perceptive enough to appreciate that the bond between mother and daughter is at least as strong as that between father and son. And how could they ever have fathomed Archy, a simple soul so deeply in love with the unattainable? Even before Cummings was murdered Randal had prepared his own death warrant when he started the relationship with Heather; he had signed it on Maddy Rigg and it was to be executed by his father at the fishing bothy: a private execution but a very public disinterment. Ruth would always wonder if the head wasn't trapped by the rubble but surfaced independently – and Archy held it back in order that it should make its appearance at the most appropriate time.